Maaya Lakshmi
The Divine Awakening

Maaya Lakshmi: The Divine Awakening

Author: Sitanshu Srivastava

ISBN: 978-93-6128-284-3 (paperback)

Copyright © 2024 by Sitanshu Srivastava

All rights reserved. No part of this publication may be reproduced, distributed, or transmitted in any form or by any means, including photocopying, recording, or other electronic or mechanical methods, without the prior written permission of the publisher, except in the case of brief quotations embodied in critical reviews and certain other noncommercial uses permitted by copyright law.

This book is available in softcover, hardcover, and Kindle edition.

First Edition: January 11th, 2024

For information about permission to reproduce selections from this book, write to author@maayalakshmi.com. This book is a work of fiction. Names, characters, places, and incidents either are products of the author's imagination or are used fictitiously. Any resemblance or intentional resemblance is covered in the Disclaimer section of the book on page (v)

About The Author

Sitanshu Srivastava, an entrepreneurial visionary, brings his creative and strategic acumen to the realm of storytelling with "Maaya Lakshmi: The Divine Awakening". A multifaceted innovator with a rich tapestry of ventures across various industries.

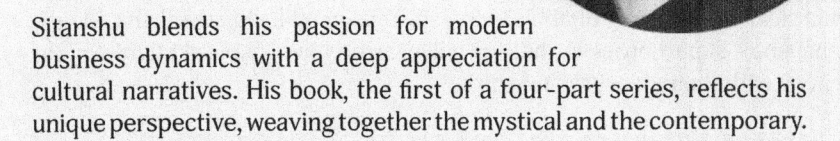

Sitanshu blends his passion for modern business dynamics with a deep appreciation for cultural narratives. His book, the first of a four-part series, reflects his unique perspective, weaving together the mystical and the contemporary.

Sitanshu's journey from managing diverse global projects to crafting compelling stories marks him as a dynamic figure shaping modern entrepreneurial and literary landscapes.

Foreword

"Maaya Lakshmi: The Divine Awakening" is a novel where Indian mythology and spirituality breathe life into a world of imagination and wonder. Through Maaya Lakshmi's eyes, a young girl destined for a remarkable journey, we explore a realm where the ordinary intertwines with the divine.

This story is more than an adventure; it's a call to recognize and celebrate equality, urging readers to respect the diverse tapestry of life. Maaya's journey from an ordinary girl to a guardian of balance is a metaphor for our own potential to rise beyond our limitations and embrace a world where differences are not just accepted but honored.

As Maaya discovers her purpose, so are we invited to reflect on ours, in a world rich with possibilities and brimming with spiritual wisdom. May this journey inspire you to see the extraordinary in the everyday and find harmony in our beautifully diverse world.

Dedication

To my loving family, cherished friends, and supportive colleagues, who have been unwavering pillars of encouragement and inspiration.

With a deep bow of respect to my parents, Mr. Suresh Kumar and Mrs. Sangeeta Srivastava, whose belief in my creative and entrepreneurial journey has been my guiding light.

This book, a fictional universe, mirrors our collective journey in decision-making and path-finding, enriched by the values and wisdom from those dear to me. A whimsical tribute to my Bhabhis - Urvashi, Shalini, Vidushi, Akanksha, Mansi, Prashansha - superheroes in their own lives, who have inspired characters in this book with their strength and spirit.

To my brothers, Sudhanshu, Saurabh, Alankar, Shashank, Shishir, Anurag, Nayan, and Naman - masters in the art of weaving these remarkable women into all our lives, adding joy and laughter to our family. To My superhero sisters, Shweta & Shiwangi. Oh the superduperheroes you are.

And to my nephews & niece, Kiaan, Shinoy, Shubh, Twira, Dakshit & Viraj, a heartfelt message: **"Grow as individuals who support and respect those around you, without discrimination. The kindness you share reflects back in countless ways. May this book inspire you to embrace diversity and make choices that lead to harmony and joy."**

With best regards

S. Srivastava

Disclaimer

This book is a work of fiction. All characters, events, and places in this novel, including those based on real locations such as Lucknow, are used fictitiously. Any resemblance to actual persons, living or dead (or transitioning between realms, whether ascending to heavenly abodes or descending into infernal depths), events, or locales is entirely coincidental and not intended by the author.

Names, characters, businesses, places, events, locales, and incidents are either the products of the author's imagination or used in a fictitious manner. The use of real place names is intended to provide a sense of setting and authenticity to the narrative but is not meant to accurately represent the actual cities, their histories, or their current conditions.

The views and opinions expressed in this novel are solely those of the author and do not represent any real individuals, organisations, religious beliefs, or philosophies. This narrative is crafted for entertainment purposes and should not be interpreted as a reflection of historical events or current realities.

Furthermore, the emotional connection that readers may develop with the characters is a natural and welcomed aspect of the reading experience, yet it remains a personal and subjective journey. Any deep attachment, fondness, or infatuation with the characters is a risk willingly undertaken by the reader and should be cherished as part of the unique magic of storytelling.

These characters, while dear to the author's heart, belong to the realm of fiction, and any semblance they bear to real individuals is purely coincidental.

Please enjoy this journey into the fictional world of "Maaya Lakshmi: The Divine Awakening," where myth and reality intertwine to create a narrative tapestry that, while unreal, resonates with the truths of the human heart.

List of characters

1. **Maaya Lakshmi**: The main protagonist, a young woman who discovers her destiny as a guardian and evolves throughout the story.
2. **Anaya**: Maaya's mentor in her journey as a guardian, offering guidance, wisdom, and support.
3. **Aarav**: A close ally of Maaya, later becoming her life partner. He plays a significant role in both her personal life and her environmental initiatives.
4. **Priya**: Maaya's best friend, offering emotional support and a sense of normalcy in Maaya's life.
5. **Dr. Vikram Singh**: Initially introduced as a visiting scholar, later revealed as an antagonist with manipulative intentions.
6. **Kaito**: A guardian from Japan, specializing in harmonizing energy flows, and an ally in the Protector's Network.
7. **Nia**: A guardian from Kenya, focused on environmental preservation and a member of the Protector's Network.
8. **The Adversary**: The main antagonist of the story, orchestrating disturbances against the natural balance.
9. **Coach Verma**: The coach of Maaya's basketball team, influencing her development in teamwork and leadership.
10. **Maaya's Family**: Briefly mentioned in the story, providing a background to Maaya's early life and values.
11. **Maaya's Protégé**: A young girl introduced in the epilogue, chosen to continue Maaya's legacy as a guardian.
12. **Members of the Protector's Network**: Various guardians from around the world who collaborate with Maaya to maintain global balance.
13. **University of Lucknow Students and Faculty**: Various characters who interact with Maaya in her academic and environmental endeavors.
14. **Local Residents of Lucknow**: Characters contributing to the story's setting and Maaya's interactions within the city.
15. **Entities of Darkness**: Supernatural adversaries that Maaya confronts in her role as a guardian.
16. **International Conference Attendees**: Individuals Maaya meets during her advocacy work on a global scale.

This list includes the main characters and groups that play significant roles in Maaya's journey, as well as peripheral figures who contribute to the narrative and world-building in "Maaya Lakshmi: The Divine Awakening."

PROLOGUE: THE AWAKENING

In the heart of ancient India, where the Ganges and Yamuna rivers entwine their fates, there lies a realm where myths breathe and legends stir. Here, in the cradle of timeless tales, the fabric of reality weaves with the threads of the fantastical, and guardians of the natural order watch over the delicate balance of the world.

As dawn broke over the city of Lucknow, painting the sky in hues of gold and crimson, a stir of energy rippled through the ancient streets. It was an energy ancient as the land itself, yet vibrant with a new awakening.

In a modest home nestled in the bustling bylanes, a young girl named Maaya Lakshmi lay dreaming. Her dreams were vivid tapestries of verdant forests and cascading rivers, where the whispers of the earth spoke in a language only her soul understood.

In these dreams, she soared as a guardian, a protector of the delicate symphony of nature.

But on this day, as the first rays of the sun touched her face, Maaya's dreams wove into a vision that transcended the boundaries of sleep. She found herself standing at the edge of a mystical forest, the air pulsating with a power both enchanting and formidable.

Before her, in a clearing bathed in ethereal light, stood three figures - embodiments of the ancient goddesses Saraswati, Durga, and Lakshmi. Their eyes, ancient and wise, bore into Maaya's, filling her with a sense of destiny. "You are chosen, Maaya Lakshmi," they spoke in unison, their voices a melody that resonated with the core of her being. "Chosen to be the guardian of balance, to protect the harmony of the natural and supernatural realms."

The Divine Awakening

As their words echoed, a surge of energy coursed through Maaya. Images flashed before her - of battles fought in shadows, of forces disrupting the harmony of the world, and of a lineage of guardians to which she now belonged.

The vision faded as quickly as it had appeared, leaving Maaya awake in her bed, the morning light streaming through her window.

Her heart raced with the remnants of the vision, the weight of her newfound destiny settling upon her young shoulders.

In the streets of Lucknow, life stirred unaware of the awakening that had occurred. A new guardian had risen, a protector born from the legacy of the ancients, ready to embark on a journey that would weave her story into the tapestry of legends.

The prologue of Maaya Lakshmi's tale had been written, not in ink, but in the destiny of the world's balance. And so began the saga of the Divine Awakening.

Contents

1. **The Unfair Game:** The significant basketball game between Maaya's University of Lucknow team and Kanpur University.
2. **Aftermath and Resolve:** Maaya copes with the consequences of the controversial game, including bullying from opposing team members.
3. **A New Challenge:** Preparation for the Inter-University State Championship, Maaya's dedication to prove her worth.
4. **The Bullying Intensifies:** Escalation of bullying from rival teams, leading to a physical confrontation.
5. **The Fall:** Maaya's fall into the Gomti River and her near-death experience.
6. **On the Brink of the Abyss:** Maaya struggles for survival in the river, reflecting on her life.
7. **Echoes of Gonda:** Flashbacks to Maaya's childhood and upbringing in Gonda.
8. **Divine Intervention:** Maaya's encounter with the guardian spirit, revealing her destiny as a guardian.
9. **A New Awakening:** Maaya embraces her new abilities and begins to understand her role as a guardian.
10. **Discovery of Powers:** Maaya explores and tests the limits of her newfound abilities.
11. **The Hidden Truth:** Maaya learns about her lineage and the legacy of guardians.
12. **Embracing the Change:** Maaya balances her university life with her responsibilities as a guardian.
13. **The Protector Emerges:** Maaya's first major act as a guardian, saving students from a construction site accident.
14. **Dual Identities:** The challenges Maaya faces in balancing her university life and secret guardian role.
15. **A Hero's Burden:** Maaya deals with the emotional and moral complexities of her dual life.
16. **Trials of the Guardian:** Maaya faces various challenges that test her powers and resolve.
17. **The Mentor:** Introduction of a mentor figure who helps Maaya understand and refine her abilities.
18. **Training and Growth:** Maaya undergoes training, honing her skills and understanding her purpose.
19. **The Shadow Looms:** Introduction of a potential antagonist or a larger threat.
20. **Confronting Darkness:** Maaya faces off against her first major adversary.
21. **Echoes of Destiny:** Maaya reflects on her journey and the larger role she's destined to play.

The Divine Awakening

22. **Alliance of Light**: Maaya forms alliances with others who can help her in her journey.
23. **A Greater Purpose**: Maaya understands her role extends beyond her immediate surroundings.
24. **Challenges of the Protector**: Maaya deals with the complexities of being a guardian.
25. **The Warrior's Path**: Maaya fully embraces her role, understanding its sacrifices and responsibilities.
26. **The First Victory**: Maaya achieves a significant victory, affirming her role as a protector.
27. **Reflections and Revelations**: Maaya reflects on her journey, understanding her destiny.
28. **Gathering Storm**: Build-up of a larger conflict or threat that Maaya must confront.
29. **The Battle Begins**: Maaya engages in a significant battle, testing her abilities.
30. **Trials of Strength and Will**: Maaya faces physical and emotional challenges.
31. **Darkness Before Dawn**: Maaya faces her darkest hour and doubts.
32. **Awakening of True Power**: Maaya discovers the full extent of her abilities.
33. **The Turning Tide**: Maaya turns the tide in a crucial conflict.
34. **The Protector's Resolve**: Maaya reaffirms her commitment to her role as a protector.
35. **Legacy of the Ancients**: Maaya learns more about the historical aspects of her powers.
36. **Alliance Against Adversity**: Maaya and her allies prepare for a final confrontation.
37. **The Final Stand**: The climax of the major conflict.
38. **Triumph of Light**: Maaya overcomes her adversary, protecting the balance.
39. **Aftermath of War**: Dealing with the aftermath of the conflict.
40. **Rebuilding and Reflection**: Maaya rebuilds her life and reflects on her journey.
41. **New Horizons**: Maaya looks towards the future and new challenges.
42. **The Protector's Network**: Establishing connections with others in her role.
43. **A Beacon of Hope**: Maaya becomes a symbol of hope and inspiration.
44. **Legacy of Maaya Lakshmi**: Reflecting on Maaya's impact and the legacy she leaves behind.

Chapter 1: The Unfair Game

In the heart of Lucknow, the University of Lucknow's basketball court was alive with anticipation. The stands were packed, a sea of faces from different colleges, all gathered for one of the most awaited matches of the season: the University of Lucknow against Kanpur University.

Maaya Lakshmi, a fresher at the University of Lucknow, laced her sneakers tightly, feeling the weight of expectation on her shoulders. Basketball was more than a game to her; it was a passion nurtured back in the narrow lanes of Gonda, her hometown. Today, it was her bridge to a dream she had long harboured – making a mark in university-level basketball.

As the game commenced, Maaya's focus was razor-sharp. She moved across the court with practiced ease, her every dribble and jump a rhythm honed by countless hours of practice. The crowd roared as she scored, her name echoing in chants that filled the air with a palpable energy.

But as the match progressed, an undercurrent of tension began to weave through the game. The Kanpur team, known for their aggressive tactics, pushed the boundaries of fair play. Fouls went uncalled, and sly elbows in the midst of the game marred the spirit of sportsmanship.

Maaya felt a surge of frustration but channelled it into her gameplay. She was a whirlwind on the court, scoring points despite the growing hostility. The final buzzer sounded, signalling a narrow and hard-fought victory for the University of Lucknow.

The win, however, was bittersweet. As Maaya shook hands with the opposing team, she couldn't miss the smirks hidden behind their sportsmanlike façade. The game, which should have been a celebration of talent and sportsmanship, had been tainted by unfair play.

Walking off the court, Maaya was engulfed by her teammates, their cheers a contrast to the turmoil inside her. The victory felt hollow, overshadowed by the unsportsmanlike conduct she had just witnessed.

That night, back in her hostel room, Maaya lay awake, staring at the ceiling. The joy of victory was eclipsed by a lingering sense of injustice. Was this what competitive sports were about? Winning at any cost?

Her mind wandered back to the open basketball courts of Gonda, where she first fell in love with the game. It was pure there, untainted by the desire to win at the expense of honour.

Maaya knew this was just the beginning of her journey in university sports. But at that moment, she made a silent vow to herself. No matter what the future held, she would play the game her way – with integrity and respect, upholding the true spirit of sportsmanship that had brought her to this court in the first place.

As sleep finally claimed her, Maaya's resolve solidified. The challenges ahead might be daunting, but she was ready to face them, staying true to the values she cherished. The game had changed for her, but so had she.

Chapter 2: Aftermath and Resolve

The morning after the game, the University of Lucknow campus was abuzz with talk about the previous night's match. For Maaya, walking through the familiar paths to her classes, the victory felt distant, like a story from another time. The whispers and congratulatory pats on the back from fellow students did little to lift the veil of introspection that had settled over her.

In the cafeteria, the animated discussion at her usual table was all about the game. "You were amazing, Maaya!" exclaimed Priya, her close friend and fellow fresher. "You totally dominated the court!"

Maaya managed a smile, but her eyes were distant. "Thanks, Priya. But it didn't feel like a real win. Not with the way Kanpur played."

Her words cast a brief shadow over the group. The excitement was tempered by the recognition of the moral dilemma they had all witnessed on the court. It was a stark reminder that the world of university sports was not just about skill and passion, but also about navigating the murky waters of ethics and integrity.

Later that day, during practice, Maaya's usual fiery presence on the court was subdued. Her coach, Mr. Verma, a seasoned veteran of the sport, noticed her lack of enthusiasm. "What's on your mind, Lakshmi?" he asked, after the session.

Maaya hesitated before sharing her thoughts about the game. Mr. Verma listened intently, nodding in understanding. "Sportsmanship is the soul of the game, Maaya. But remember, you can't control how others play. You can only control how you respond. Use this as a learning experience, not just for basketball, but for life."

His words resonated with Maaya, offering a perspective she hadn't considered. It was about responding, not reacting. About holding onto her values, even when others let go of theirs.

The following week brought a new challenge. News came that the University of Lucknow was scheduled to play a rematch with Kanpur University, this time on Kanpur's home ground. The announcement reignited the discussions about the previous game's fairness, and the anticipation for the rematch was tinged with apprehension.

Maaya felt a mix of emotions as the day of the game approached. There was a part of her that dreaded going back onto the court with the Kanpur team, knowing their playstyle. But there was also a stronger part, a determined part, that wanted to rise above the pettiness and show that integrity could triumph over underhanded tactics.

The journey to Kanpur was a quiet one. Maaya sat by the window, her thoughts a whirlwind. She remembered her early days playing basketball in Gonda, the pure joy of the game, and her dreams of playing at higher levels. She realized that this was part of that journey – facing challenges, both physical and moral, and overcoming them.

The game in Kanpur was intense from the start. The home crowd was vociferous in their support for their team, and the atmosphere was charged. Maaya stepped onto the court with a renewed sense of purpose. This time, she was ready, not just to play, but to lead by example.
As the game progressed, Maaya's resolve showed in her every move. She played with a focus and a grace that seemed to elevate not just her performance but also the spirit of the game. The Kanpur team's tactics were still aggressive, but Maaya and her team responded with skilful play, not aggression.

In the end, it was a close game, but Lucknow emerged victorious once again. This time, however, the victory felt different to Maaya. It wasn't just about scoring more points; it was about proving a point – that integrity and skill could go hand in hand.

Walking off the court, amidst the cheering and the congratulations, Maaya felt a sense of satisfaction. She had not only confronted her doubts but had also overcome them. She had stayed true to her values, and in doing so, had found a deeper understanding of what it meant to be a sportsperson.

That night, as Maaya lay in her hostel bed, she felt a sense of peace. The journey ahead would undoubtedly be filled with more challenges, but she knew now that she had the strength to face them, on and off the court. Her love for basketball had brought her here, but her commitment to sportsmanship would guide her forward.

Chapter 3: A New Challenge

The aftermath of the rematch with Kanpur University had left a lasting impression on Maaya. Her performance on the court had not only demonstrated her athletic prowess but also solidified her commitment to playing with integrity. As the buzz from the game subsided, a new challenge emerged on the horizon – the Inter-University State Championship, slated to be held in Lucknow.

The championship was more than just another tournament for Maaya; it was an opportunity to showcase her talent on a larger stage and to test her resolve under even more competitive and high-pressure conditions. The thought of it filled her with a mix of excitement and nervous anticipation.

Training sessions became more rigorous in the weeks leading up to the championship. Maaya found herself pushing her limits, driven by a desire to excel not just for personal glory but for the pride of her university. Her coach, Mr. Verma, noticed her heightened dedication. "You're setting a high bar, Lakshmi," he remarked one evening after practice. "Keep this up, and you'll make a mark in the state championship."

Maaya's response was a determined nod. She knew that the upcoming championship would bring tougher opponents and more complex dynamics on the court. But she was ready to face them, armed with her skills and her unwavering spirit.

As the days passed, Maaya's thoughts often drifted back to her hometown of Gonda. She remembered the open basketball courts where she first fell in love with the game, the cheers of her childhood friends, and the endless support of her family. Those memories were a constant source of strength and motivation, reminding her of why she played the game.

The night before the championship, Maaya lay in her bed, unable to sleep. The excitement was palpable, but so was the pressure. She thought about the journey that had brought her here – from playing in the dusty courts of Gonda to competing in one of the most prestigious basketball tournaments in the state.

Her mind replayed every dribble, every shot, and every game that had shaped her as a player. She thought about her teammates, her coach, and her family – all of whom had played a part in her journey. It wasn't just her skill that had brought her here; it was a collective effort, a shared dream.

The morning of the championship dawned bright and clear. The University of Lucknow campus was abuzz with activity, with teams from various universities arriving, each eager to claim the title. The air was thick with anticipation, and the stakes were high.

Maaya stepped onto the court with a sense of purpose. She looked at her teammates, seeing the same determination in their eyes. They were not just a team; they were a unit, bound by a common goal.

As the games commenced, Maaya played with a passion that was infectious. Her movements were fluid, her strategies sharp, and her focus unwavering. She led her team through each game, her performance a blend of skill and heart.

The matches were intense, each team bringing their best to the court. Maaya faced challenges she hadn't encountered before – strategic plays, formidable opponents, and moments of doubt. But with each challenge, she rose, adapting and overcoming, her spirit undeterred.

The championship progressed, and the University of Lucknow

team found themselves advancing through the rounds. Each victory was a testament to their hard work, their synergy, and their collective desire to succeed.

Finally, it was the day of the finals. The stadium was packed, the atmosphere electric. Maaya took a moment to absorb it all – the cheers, the anticipation, the sense of being part of something significant.

As the final game began, Maaya felt every ounce of her training, her experiences, and her dreams converging. This was her moment, her opportunity to shine. And she played, not just with her body, but with her soul.

The game was a battle of skill and will. Each team gave it their all, but in the end, it was the University of Lucknow that emerged victorious. The crowd erupted in cheers, and Maaya's heart soared with joy.

Standing on the court, holding the championship trophy, Maaya knew that this was more than just a win. It was a validation of her journey, a recognition of her hard work, and a tribute to the game she loved.

As the team celebrated, Maaya's eyes searched the stands, finding her family cheering for her, pride evident in their eyes. In that moment, she knew that no matter where her journey took her, her heart would always remain rooted in the courts of Gonda, where a young girl's dream had taken flight.

Chapter 4: The Bullying Intensifies

The victory at the Inter-University State Championship had put Maaya and her team in the spotlight, a recognition that brought both pride and unwanted attention. As the euphoria of the win subsided, Maaya faced a resurgence of an old challenge – bullying from rival teams, now intensified by her rising prominence.

The first incident occurred on a seemingly ordinary day at the university. As Maaya walked through the campus, she overheard hushed whispers and saw pointing fingers – subtle signs that something was amiss. It didn't take long for the whispers to turn into outright confrontations.

One afternoon, while leaving the library, Maaya was accosted by a group of students from a rival university. Their leader, a tall, imposing figure, stepped forward with a sneer. "So, you think you're some kind of star now, huh, Maaya?" he taunted. "Just remember, stars can fall just as quickly as they rise."

Maaya, taken aback by the hostility, tried to walk away, but the group blocked her path. The verbal jabs continued, each word laced with envy and malice. It was clear that her success on the court had made her a target.

The encounters became more frequent and more aggressive. During practice sessions, Maaya would often find derogatory graffiti sprayed on her locker and hostile glares from players of other teams. The basketball court, once her sanctuary, began to feel like a battleground.

Maaya tried to handle the situation with the same grace and resilience she showed on the court. She confided in her coach and her teammates, who rallied around her, offering support and solidarity. But the constant negativity started to take a toll on her.

The situation reached a crescendo one evening after a practice match. As Maaya was heading home, she was cornered by a group from the rival team. What started as verbal taunts quickly escalated into a physical altercation. Maaya found herself pushed against a wall, her basketball snatched away and tossed aside.

The physicality of the confrontation was a shock, but it was the betrayal of the sportsman spirit that hurt Maaya the most. She had always viewed basketball as a game of respect, a field where rivalry was healthy and constructive. But this was something else, something darker.

That night, as Maaya nursed a bruised arm and a bruised spirit, she realized that the challenges she faced were not just on the court but off it as well. The bullying was a test of her character, a trial that she had to face and overcome.

Determined not to be intimidated, Maaya resolved to stand up against the bullying. She reported the incidents to the university authorities, who promised to take action. She also spoke openly about her experiences, refusing to be silenced by fear.

In the days that followed, Maaya's stance became a topic of discussion on campus. Her courage in facing the bullies head-on inspired others who had faced similar harassment. Slowly, the tide began to turn. The support for Maaya grew, overshadowing the negativity.
The experience taught Maaya a crucial lesson – that strength was not just about physical prowess, but also about the courage to stand up for what is right. It reinforced her belief in the power of integrity and resilience.

As Maaya lay in bed, reflecting on the recent events, she felt a renewed sense of purpose. The challenges she faced were not going to deter her; they were going to make her stronger. She was Maaya Lakshmi, a basketball player, a student, and now, a fighter in her own right.

Chapter 5: The Fall

The weeks following the confrontation with her bullies were a time of introspection for Maaya. She continued to excel in basketball, but the incidents had left a shadow over her once-unbridled joy for the game. The campus, with its ivy-covered buildings and bustling corridors, felt different now; it was as if every corner held a whisper of the challenges she had faced.

Maaya's resolve, however, remained unshaken. She threw herself into her studies and training with a renewed vigour, finding solace in the routine and the support of her friends and teammates. Yet, the undercurrent of tension from the bullying incidents lingered.

One fateful evening, as the sun dipped below the horizon, casting a golden glow over the University of Lucknow, Maaya found herself alone, practicing on the outdoor court. The rhythmic bounce of the basketball on the concrete was a soothing sound, a reminder of simpler times.

Lost in her thoughts, Maaya didn't notice the group approaching until they were almost upon her. It was the same group of bullies, their expressions a mix of malice and determination. Maaya's heart sank; she had hoped that the worst was behind her.

The confrontation was swift and unexpected. Words turned into shoves, and in the heat of the moment, Maaya found herself pushed backwards. She stumbled, losing her balance, and in a split second, her world turned upside down.

Maaya's fall seemed to happen in slow motion. She felt the air rush past her as she tumbled towards the river Gomti, which ran along the edge of the campus. Her thoughts were a blur – a mix of disbelief, fear, and a deep sense of injustice.

With a splash that echoed in the quiet evening, Maaya hit the water. The coldness of the river was a shock to her system, and for a moment, she was disoriented, struggling to understand what had just happened.

Instinctively, Maaya fought to surface, but her movements were hampered by the weight of her clothes and the shock of the cold water. Panic set in as she realized that she was in trouble, that this was not just another challenge to overcome – this was a fight for survival.
As she struggled in the water, Maaya's thoughts turned to her family, her friends, and the dreams she had yet to fulfil. The idea of her journey ending in the dark, cold depths of the Gomti was unbearable.

But as Maaya fought to stay afloat, her strength began to wane. The river, with its relentless current, seemed to be pulling her under, claiming her as its own. In those desperate moments, Maaya's life flashed before her eyes – the basketball courts of Gonda, the cheers of victory, the faces of those she loved.

Just when it seemed like the river would claim her, Maaya thought of her last game, the feel of the basketball in her hands, the sound of her name being chanted. It was a reminder of who she was – a fighter, a dreamer, a survivor.

With a renewed burst of energy, Maaya fought against the current, her arms pushing through the water with all the strength she could muster. She was Maaya Lakshmi, and she was not going to let her story end here, not in the depths of the Gomti.

But as the darkness closed in and her strength faded, Maaya realized that this was a battle she might not win. Her thoughts turned to a silent prayer, a plea for a chance to continue her

The Divine Awakening

journey, to fulfil her destiny.

And then, just as the darkness threatened to engulf her completely, a strange calm descended upon Maaya. It was as if the river itself was responding to her plea, holding her in a gentle embrace. In that moment, on the brink of consciousness, Maaya felt a presence, a sense of being watched over by something greater than herself.

It was in this moment, suspended between life and death, that Maaya's true journey began – a journey that would take her beyond the realms of the ordinary, into the heart of her destiny.

Chapter 6: On the Brink of the Abyss

Submerged in the chilling embrace of the Gomti River, Maaya Lakshmi found herself caught between the realms of consciousness and oblivion. The muffled sounds of the world above water were a distant echo, fading against the relentless rush of the river.

In those terrifying moments, Maaya's life seemed to hang by a fragile thread, each second stretching into eternity. Panic and fear battled with her will to survive. Her limbs, once agile and powerful on the basketball court, now flailed desperately in the unyielding grip of the river.

Images of her life in Gonda flashed through her mind – the open fields where she played as a child, the warmth of her family home, and the countless evenings spent practicing basketball, each shot a step closer to her dreams. These memories were now like beacons in the dark, urging her to fight, to cling to life.

As Maaya struggled, her thoughts turned to her parents. The pride in their eyes after every game, their unwavering support, and their dreams for her future – all these became a source of strength, a reason to keep fighting. She couldn't let her story end here, not when there was so much left to live for, so much left to achieve.

But as the seconds ticked by, Maaya's strength waned. The cold of the river seeped into her bones, sapping her energy, pulling her deeper into despair. In a fleeting moment of clarity amidst the chaos, Maaya realized the grim reality – she might not make it out of the river alive.

It was then, in the depths of despair and exhaustion, that something extraordinary happened. A warm sensation began to spread through Maaya's body, a stark contrast to the icy waters around her. It was as if an invisible force was infusing her with energy, with life.

Maaya's mind, clouded by the fear of drowning, struggled to comprehend this new sensation. Was it her mind playing tricks, a last burst of adrenaline, or something beyond her understanding? In her weakened state, she couldn't tell. All she knew was that it gave her a flicker of hope, a chance to fight back against the seemingly inevitable.

With this newfound energy, Maaya pushed against the current, her arms slicing through the water with renewed vigour. Each stroke was a defiance against fate, a refusal to succumb to the abyss. The surface, once a distant dream, now seemed within reach.

As she neared the surface, gasping for air, Maaya's senses returned in a rush. The sounds of the night, the lights from the distant shore, and the taste of fresh air were overwhelming in their intensity. She had made it; she was alive.

Collapsed on the riverbank, coughing and shivering, Maaya looked up at the night sky. The stars seemed to shine brighter, and the world felt different, as if she had crossed a threshold into a new existence.

Exhausted but alive, Maaya lay there, trying to make sense of what had happened. How had she survived? What was that strange warmth that had coursed through her in the river's depths? Questions swirled in her mind, but one thing was clear – her life had been changed forever.

In that moment of solitude, Maaya Lakshmi, the basketball player from Gonda, realized that her journey was about to take a turn into the unknown. The river had not only tested her will to live but had also awakened something within her, something powerful and mysterious.

As she slowly got to her feet, Maaya knew that the road ahead would be fraught with challenges and revelations. But she was ready. The girl who had fallen into the Gomti was not the same one who had emerged. A new chapter in her life had begun, and with it, the awakening of a destiny beyond her wildest dreams.

Chapter 7: Echoes of Gonda

The days following Maaya's harrowing experience in the Gomti River were filled with reflection and recuperation. She found herself frequently revisiting the memories of her childhood in Gonda, a small town where her love for basketball first took root. These reflections were not just a journey into the past; they seemed to hold keys to understanding the present, especially after her near-death experience.

Gonda, with its wide-open fields and close-knit community, had always been a place where dreams felt attainable. Maaya remembered the old basketball hoop in her backyard, slightly rusted but standing tall – a symbol of her early aspirations. It was here that her father had taught her the basics of the game, turning each evening into a lesson in both sports and life.

Her parents, always supportive, had been her pillars. Her father, a high school teacher, was a quiet man of great integrity, while her mother, a local librarian, was a wellspring of stories and encouragement. Their belief in her had been unwavering, a constant source of strength.

As Maaya lay in her bed in Lucknow, recuperating, she couldn't help but feel a deep sense of gratitude for her upbringing. The values instilled in her – resilience, fairness, and the pursuit of excellence – had been her guiding stars, leading her to this point.

But now, there was a new element in her life, something unexplained and profound. The incident in the river had left her with more than just a renewed appreciation for life; it had awakened a strange, almost mystical sensation within her. It was as if the waters of the Gomti had unlocked something dormant, something that was now a part of her very being.

In the quiet hours of the night, Maaya would often sit by her window, gazing at the stars, feeling the echo of that mysterious warmth that had saved her in the river. She wondered if it was merely her imagination, a trick of a stressed mind, or if it was something more, something real and powerful.

Her return to the basketball court was a tentative one. As she dribbled and shot, Maaya couldn't shake off the feeling that she was different now. The game, which had always been her refuge and joy, now felt like a reminder of the questions that hung over her.

One evening, as she practiced alone, Maaya experienced a moment that would forever change her understanding of what had happened in the river. As she leaped for a particularly challenging shot, time seemed to slow down. The sensation from the river returned, but this time it was accompanied by a clarity and a sense of control.

Maaya landed gracefully, the ball passing perfectly through the hoop. She stood there, stunned, realizing that what she had just felt was no illusion. It was real, tangible, and incredible. The realization sent a thrill through her – she had somehow been changed by her experience in the river, granted an ability that defied explanation.

In the days that followed, Maaya began to experiment with this newfound ability, testing its limits and learning to harness it. It was a process filled with awe and apprehension. She knew she had to keep it a secret, at least until she understood it better. The last thing she wanted was to attract more attention, especially the kind that had led to the incident with the bullies.

But with this secret came isolation. Maaya found herself pulling away from her friends and teammates, fearing that her new abilities would somehow put them in danger or alienate her from them. The weight of this secret was a heavy one, and Maaya struggled to bear it alone.

As she lay in bed each night, Maaya would think back to Gonda, to the simplicity and purity of her dreams back then. Now, those dreams seemed to have entwined with something much larger and more mysterious. She was still Maaya Lakshmi, the girl from Gonda, but she was also something more now – something extraordinary.

Chapter 8: Divine Intervention

In the stillness of her room, with the moon casting a soft glow through the window, Maaya wrestled with the reality of her newfound abilities. They were both exhilarating and daunting, a secret that she guarded closely. Yet, with each passing day, the urge to understand the source and extent of these abilities grew stronger.

It was a week after her return to the basketball court that Maaya experienced an event that would significantly alter her understanding of the changes she was undergoing. As she walked along the banks of the Gomti River, the site of her near-fatal fall, she felt a strange pull, an unspoken call that resonated deep within her.
Standing by the river, Maaya closed her eyes and allowed the sensations to wash over her. The gentle lapping of the water, the rustling of leaves in the gentle breeze, and the distant hum of the city all merged into a symphony of the night. It was here, in this serene setting, that Maaya first sensed her connection to something beyond the ordinary, a link to a realm that defied logic.

As she opened her eyes, Maaya was greeted by an astonishing sight. Before her stood a figure, ethereal and radiant, emanating a soft light that seemed to dance with the night. The figure was a woman, her features noble and her gaze piercing, yet filled with kindness.

Maaya's breath caught in her throat. She instinctively knew that this was no ordinary encounter. The woman before her exuded a presence that was both comforting and awe-inspiring.

"Do not fear, Maaya," the woman spoke, her voice like a melody that soothed Maaya's tumultuous thoughts. "I am here to guide you, to help you understand the gift you have been bestowed."

Maaya listened, spellbound, as the woman revealed herself to be a guardian spirit, a protector of the natural order, linked to the sacred waters of the Gomti. She explained that Maaya's near-death experience in the river was a catalyst for awakening the latent abilities within her, abilities that were part of a much larger design.

"You have been chosen, Maaya, for a purpose far greater than you can imagine. Your strength, your integrity, and your courage have made you the ideal guardian of balance. But with this gift comes responsibility," the spirit continued, her eyes locking onto Maaya's with an intensity that held the weight of the world.

Maaya, overwhelmed by the revelation, felt a surge of questions rise within her. "Why me? What am I supposed to do with these abilities?"

"The path will reveal itself in time," the spirit answered. "Your journey is not just about harnessing these abilities, but about understanding the balance between the ordinary and the extraordinary. You must use your gift to protect, to heal, and to maintain harmony."

As the spirit spoke, images flashed through Maaya's mind — visions of potential challenges and conflicts, of her standing as a beacon against forces that threatened to disrupt the natural balance.

The encounter ended as swiftly as it began, with the spirit fading into the night, leaving Maaya alone by the river once again. But the air around her felt different now, charged with a sense of purpose.

Maaya walked back to her hostel, her mind racing with the enormity of what she had just learned. She was no longer just a student and an athlete; she was now a guardian, chosen for a role that intertwined with the mystical forces of nature.

Lying in bed, Maaya knew that her life had irrevocably changed. Ahead of her lay a path filled with challenges and wonders beyond her wildest imaginations. But for the first time, she felt a sense of clarity about the strange abilities she had acquired. She was ready to embark on this new journey, to embrace her destiny as a protector, a guardian anointed by the divine.

Chapter 9: A New Awakening

In the days that followed her mystical encounter by the river, Maaya's perception of the world around her began to shift. The campus of the University of Lucknow, with its bustling students and ancient trees, seemed both familiar and extraordinary. Maaya found herself seeing the ordinary with new eyes, sensing the undercurrents of energy and life that flowed around her.

Her newfound abilities, once a source of confusion and fear, now felt like an integral part of her being. She began to experiment discreetly, testing the limits of her powers. In the solitude of her room or in secluded corners of the campus, Maaya discovered she could manipulate energies, sense the emotions of those around her, and even, to her astonishment, heal minor ailments with a touch.

Each discovery was a piece of the puzzle, fitting into the larger picture the guardian spirit had revealed to her. Maaya realized that her role as a guardian was not just about using her powers; it was about understanding the balance between the human and the mystical, the seen and the unseen.

The basketball court became a place of solace and empowerment for Maaya. Here, she felt most connected to her dual identity. The physicality of the game, the teamwork, and the strategy were now complemented by her heightened senses and intuition. Maaya played with a grace and intensity that inspired her teammates and captivated spectators.

But with great power came great responsibility. Maaya knew she couldn't reveal her abilities to the world. The fear of being misunderstood, of being seen as different, weighed heavily on her. She confided only in her diary, pouring her thoughts and experiences onto its pages, her silent confidante.

One evening, as Maaya walked through the quieter parts of the campus, she felt a sudden surge of energy. Her instincts led her to a secluded alley, where she found a stray dog, injured and whimpering in pain. Maaya approached cautiously, extending her hand. As she touched the dog, she focused her energy, feeling the flow from her palm to the animal.

To her amazement, the wound began to heal, the pain in the dog's eyes easing. Maaya felt a deep connection with the creature, a bond that transcended species. It was a profound moment, a realization of her ability to heal and protect beyond the human realm.

In the following weeks, Maaya continued to embrace her role as a guardian. She intervened in small ways, preventing accidents, aiding injured animals, and subtly using her powers to help those in need. Each act, though minor, reinforced her commitment to her new path.

However, with this awakening came a sense of isolation. Maaya felt distant from her friends, who remained unaware of the changes she had undergone. She longed to share her experiences but feared the consequences of revealing her true self.

As the university year progressed, Maaya's double life became her new normal. She excelled in her studies and basketball, while secretly honing her abilities, learning to balance the mundane with the extraordinary.
But as Maaya grew more confident in her role as a guardian, she sensed that the challenges she had faced so far were just the beginning. The world was vast, and the balance she was sworn to protect was fragile. Unknown to her, forces were stirring, currents shifting, setting the stage for greater trials and tests of her resolve.

The Divine Awakening

Maaya's journey as a guardian had just begun, and the path ahead was filled with uncertainty and danger. But she was ready, armed with her powers and guided by a sense of duty that transcended her own desires. She was Maaya Lakshmi, the girl from Gonda, the basketball champion, and now, a protector of the delicate balance of life.

Chapter 10: Discovery of Powers

The transformation from a university athlete to a guardian of a hidden realm was not an easy path for Maaya. With each passing day, she found herself delving deeper into the mysteries of her newfound abilities. The campus and the city of Lucknow, once familiar terrains, now became the grounds for her secret explorations and learning.

Maaya dedicated her nights to understanding the extent of her powers. She discovered she could sense disturbances in the natural energy around her, a skill that allowed her to be at the right place at the right time to avert minor mishaps or accidents. Her intuition had sharpened, giving her an almost precognitive understanding of situations.

One night, under the veil of darkness, Maaya tested her abilities further in the open fields near the university. She focused her energy, feeling the power coursing through her veins, and to her amazement, she found she could manipulate the elements around her. Leaves rustled and swirled at her command, and the wind whispered secrets as it passed by her.

As she practiced, Maaya realized that her powers were not just physical manifestations but were deeply connected to her emotions and intentions. When she was calm and focused, her control was precise. But when doubts and fears clouded her mind, her powers became erratic and unpredictable. This revelation made her understand the importance of balance, not just in her abilities but in her mind and spirit.

However, with great power came great questions. Maaya grappled with the moral implications of her abilities. She understood that she held a significant responsibility and that her actions, no matter how well-intentioned, could have consequences.

Her solitary experiments were interrupted one evening by an unexpected encounter. While practicing in a secluded part of the campus, Maaya was found by Priya, who had been looking for her. The shock and confusion on Priya's face were evident as she stumbled upon Maaya in the midst of manipulating the energy around her.

Confronted with the possibility of revealing her secret, Maaya felt a surge of panic. But looking into Priya's wide, fearful eyes, she knew she had to trust her friend. With a deep breath, Maaya decided to confide in Priya, revealing the truth about her abilities and the encounter by the river.

Priya listened in awe and disbelief as Maaya recounted her experiences. The revelation brought them closer, with Priya becoming the first person to know about Maaya's dual life. She promised to keep Maaya's secret, offering support and a listening ear.

As the days turned into weeks, Maaya continued to juggle her life as a student and basketball player with her secret role as a guardian. Her relationship with Priya deepened, providing her with much-needed companionship and understanding in her otherwise solitary journey.

But as Maaya grew more adept with her powers, she felt an undercurrent of change in the air. It was as if her actions had set off ripples in the fabric of the ordinary world. Unbeknownst to her, her activities had started to attract attention, not just from those who watched over the balance of the natural world but also from those who sought to disrupt it.

Maaya was on the brink of a new chapter in her life, one that would take her beyond the confines of her university life and into the broader canvas of cosmic balance and conflict. The journey ahead was fraught with challenges and dangers, but Maaya, with her powers and her unwavering spirit, was ready to face whatever lay ahead.

Chapter 11: The Hidden Truth

As Maaya navigated her new reality, balancing her life as a university student and a burgeoning guardian, she couldn't shake off the feeling that there was more to her abilities and her role than she had uncovered. The questions that lingered in her mind led her on a quest for answers.

One crisp autumn evening, Maaya revisited the Gomti River, the site of her transformation. The river flowed quietly, its waters reflecting the starlit sky. Maaya stood at the water's edge, hoping to connect with the guardian spirit who had first revealed her destiny.

To her surprise and relief, the ethereal figure emerged from the shimmering waters, her presence as calming and majestic as before. "You seek answers, Maaya," the spirit said, her voice echoing gently around them.

Maaya nodded, her heart racing with anticipation. "Who am I really? Why was I chosen? What is the true extent of my powers?" The questions tumbled out, each a reflection of the turmoil within her.

The spirit gazed at Maaya, a hint of empathy in her ageless eyes. "Your journey is not just a result of chance. It is the culmination of a legacy, a lineage that dates back centuries. You, Maaya, are the descendant of a line of guardians, chosen ones who have protected the balance of nature and humanity."

Maaya listened, awestruck, as the spirit recounted the history of the guardians, a lineage of individuals blessed with extraordinary abilities to protect and maintain the equilibrium between the natural and the supernatural. Each guardian's powers were unique, manifesting based on their deepest traits and strengths.

"The powers you possess are a reflection of your inner self – your integrity, your courage, and your compassion. They are gifts, but they also come with a responsibility to use them for the greater good," the spirit explained.

The revelation was overwhelming. Maaya felt a sense of pride, but also a weight of responsibility. She was part of something ancient and significant, a legacy that transcended her individual existence.

"But why now? Why reveal this to me at this point in my life?" Maaya asked, seeking to understand the timing of her awakening.

"The world is in a state of flux, a period where the balance is threatened. Your awakening was triggered by the need for a new guardian, one who could rise to the challenges of the present day. Your near drowning in the Gomti was no accident; it was a catalyst, chosen by fate to awaken your powers," the spirit responded.

As the conversation progressed, Maaya felt a growing sense of purpose. She understood that her journey was not a solitary one. She was part of a continuum, a chain of guardians whose actions had shaped history in ways unseen and unsung.

The spirit's final words to Maaya were a call to action. "Your journey is your own, Maaya, but know that you are never alone. Trust in your powers, and when the time comes, trust in your heart. It will lead you to where you are needed most."
As the spirit disappeared into the river, Maaya stood silently, processing the enormity of the revelation. She felt empowered and humbled, aware of the path that lay ahead.

Returning to her daily life, Maaya now saw everything through a

The Divine Awakening

different lens. Her interactions, her decisions, even her basketball games, took on new meaning. She was not just Maaya Lakshmi, the university student, and athlete; she was a guardian, a protector of a legacy that stretched back through the ages.

Chapter 12: Embracing the Change

In the wake of her revelation, Maaya's days at the University of Lucknow took on a new dimension. With the knowledge of her legacy as a guardian, every moment felt charged with purpose. Her interactions with friends and peers, once ordinary, now carried an undercurrent of her secret identity. Maaya walked the campus with a new sense of determination, aware of the unseen balance she was sworn to protect.

Despite the weight of her newfound responsibility, Maaya found a sense of liberation in embracing her role. Her abilities, once a source of confusion and fear, were now integral to her identity. She continued to hone her skills in secret, finding solace in the quiet corners of the campus where she could practice undisturbed.

Her nightly forays into the world of her powers revealed more about her capabilities. She found she could sense disturbances in the natural order, a skill that allowed her to be a silent guardian, correcting minor imbalances before they escalated. With each intervention, Maaya grew more confident in her role, finding a rhythm in her dual life.

The basketball court remained her sanctuary, where she could blend in as just another player. Yet, even here, her abilities seeped through. Her reflexes were sharper, her intuition about the flow of the game more acute. Basketball was no longer just a game; it was a dance of energy, a physical expression of her inner power.

However, with great power came a sense of isolation. Maaya struggled with the burden of her secret, the knowledge that she was different. She longed to share her experiences with her teammates and friends, especially Priya, who had become her confidante. But the fear of being misunderstood, of alienating herself from those she cared about, kept her silent.

As the semester progressed, Maaya found herself at the centre of an unexpected incident that would test her resolve. A fire broke out in one of the university buildings, a blaze that threatened to engulf the structure. As students and faculty panicked, Maaya's instincts as a guardian kicked in.

Amidst the chaos, she slipped away, using her abilities to aid in the evacuation unseen. Her subtle manipulation of energies helped guide students to safety, extinguishing small fires and clearing paths through the smoke-filled corridors.

The fire was eventually controlled, but the incident left a profound impact on Maaya. She realized the extent of her powers, and more importantly, the difference she could make. It was a poignant reminder of the spirit's words – her role was to protect, to maintain harmony.

In the aftermath of the fire, as the university community came together to heal, Maaya felt a deep connection to the people around her. She understood that her journey as a guardian was not just about grand gestures of heroism. It was about the small acts of kindness, the subtle interventions that kept the balance.

As she lay in bed that night, Maaya reflected on her journey. She had come a long way from the basketball courts of Gonda. She had faced challenges, both personal and supernatural, and had emerged stronger. Her path as a guardian was just beginning, but she was ready to embrace it fully, with all its trials and triumphs. Maaya Lakshmi, the university student, the basketball player, was now also a guardian of the unseen world. It was a role she accepted with humility and determination, ready to face whatever lay ahead in the journey of her extraordinary destiny.

Chapter 13: The Protector Emerges

Maaya's life at the University of Lucknow continued to evolve as she embraced her identity as a guardian. The campus, with its blend of academic rigor and youthful energy, became a backdrop to her secret mission of maintaining balance and protecting those around her.

As the weeks passed, Maaya's confidence in her abilities grew. She found herself more attuned to the subtle shifts in the world around her, sensing disturbances before they manifested. Her nights were spent patrolling the campus and the surrounding areas, a silent sentinel safeguarding the peace.

It was during one of these nightly vigils that Maaya faced her first significant challenge as a guardian. A group of students, lost in the thrill of a dare, found themselves in a dangerous situation near an old construction site on the campus outskirts. The unstable structure posed a grave risk, and the students' laughter soon turned to cries for help as part of the building collapsed, trapping them.

Maaya, sensing the disruption, rushed to the site. Hidden in the shadows, she assessed the situation. Time was of the essence; she had to act fast. Harnessing her abilities, Maaya began to carefully manipulate the energies around the collapsed structure, creating a passage for the students to escape.

One by one, the trapped students emerged, bewildered but unharmed. They spoke of feeling a strange presence, a comforting force that guided them out of the darkness. Rumours began to circulate about a guardian angel watching over the university.
The incident at the construction site was a turning point for Maaya. It reinforced the reality of her new life and the impact she

could have. While she remained a hidden figure in the rescue, the sense of accomplishment and purpose she felt was undeniable.

Back on the basketball court, Maaya continued to shine. Her experiences as a guardian began to subtly influence her gameplay. She played with a newfound intuition and grace; her movements almost predictive. Her team, inspired by her leadership, reached new heights, their success a source of joy and pride for the university.

However, Maaya's double life began to take a toll on her. Juggling academics, basketball, and her duties as a guardian left her with little time for herself or her friends. Priya, ever perceptive, noticed the change in Maaya. "You're pushing yourself too hard," she cautioned, concern evident in her voice.

Maaya offered a reassuring smile, but deep down, she knew Priya was right. The burden of her secret was heavy, and the fear of exposure was constant. Yet, the sense of duty she felt as a guardian left her no choice but to continue.

As Maaya lay in bed one night, reflecting on her journey, she realized that her life had irrevocably changed. The simplicity of her earlier days at the university seemed like a distant memory. Now, she lived in a world where her actions had far-reaching consequences, a world that required her to be vigilant, brave, and selfless.

The path of a guardian was a solitary one, but Maaya was determined to walk it. She had been chosen for this role, and she would fulfil it to the best of her abilities. The protector in her had emerged, and there was no turning back.

Chapter 14: Dual Identities

As the winter semester at the University of Lucknow progressed, Maaya found herself increasingly living a life of contrasts. By day, she was a prominent figure on the basketball court, her prowess and leadership skills earning her accolades and admiration. Her academic life, too, was a testament to her dedication and intelligence. But as night fell, she embraced a different role – that of a silent guardian, using her extraordinary abilities to maintain harmony and protect the unsuspecting.

This dual existence, however, was not without its challenges. Maaya often felt the strain of her secret life. The solitude of her nightly endeavours stood in stark contrast to her daytime persona, where she was surrounded by friends and teammates. The weight of her responsibilities as a guardian sometimes clashed with the simpler joys of her university life.

The biggest challenge Maaya faced was keeping her secret identity hidden from those closest to her. Priya, her best friend and confidante, sensed the change in her but respected Maaya's privacy. Their friendship, strong as it was, now had an unspoken boundary, one that Maaya dared not cross for fear of endangering Priya or compromising her role as a guardian.

One evening, the delicate balance Maaya had been maintaining was threatened. A major cultural festival at the university saw the campus come alive with lights, music, and celebrations. Maaya, participating in the basketball exhibition match, was the star of the evening. The crowd cheered as she led her team to a spectacular win.

But amidst the celebrations, Maaya's heightened senses picked up a disturbance. A group of students, wandering beyond the safety of the lit areas, had unwittingly ventured into a hazardous part of the campus, where old, unused buildings posed a serious risk.

Torn between her desire to join her friends in the post-match celebrations and her duty as a guardian, Maaya made a swift decision. Making an excuse about needing some fresh air, she slipped away from the festivities and headed towards the danger.

Using her abilities, Maaya navigated the treacherous terrain, guiding the students back to safety. Her intervention was subtle, and the students remained unaware of the guiding force that had averted their potential peril. Once certain of their safety, Maaya returned to the festival, her absence unnoticed in the revelry.

This incident, however, left Maaya with a profound realization. The line between her two worlds was blurring, and the risk of her secret being exposed was growing. She understood that with each passing day, the complexity of her life as a guardian would only increase.

Maaya also began to feel the emotional toll of her dual identity. The loneliness of her secret mission, the constant vigilance, and the fear of discovery weighed heavily on her. She longed for the simplicity of her earlier days at the university, yet she knew that her life could never return to that normalcy.

As she lay in bed that night, Maaya reflected on the path she had chosen. It was a path of shadows and light, of solitude and responsibility. But it was also a path of purpose and power. Maaya knew that her journey as a guardian was just beginning, and she was prepared to walk it, no matter the challenges it brought.

Chapter 15: A Hero's Burden

The duality of Maaya's life at the University of Lucknow continued to be a source of internal conflict. As the winter semester gave way to spring, the campus bloomed with new life, mirroring the evolution of Maaya's journey. However, with each passing day, the burden of her secret grew heavier, a constant companion amid her academic and athletic successes.

Maaya's role as a guardian brought with it not just physical challenges but moral dilemmas. She grappled with questions of right and wrong, of when to intervene and when to step back. Her powers, though a gift, often felt like a heavy mantle she had reluctantly accepted. The joy of helping others was frequently overshadowed by the fear of the potential consequences of her actions.

As Maaya's sense of isolation deepened, she found herself withdrawing from her friends, including Priya. Conversations that were once filled with laughter and plans for the future now felt strained, the unspoken truth creating a barrier that Maaya couldn't cross. She longed to share her experiences with Priya, to unburden her soul, but the risk was too great.

The basketball court remained her only refuge, where she could blend her two identities. Here, Maaya channelled her frustrations and doubts into the game, her performance reaching new heights. Yet, even in these moments of triumph, her secret loomed large, a shadow that never quite receded.

The true test of Maaya's resolve came unexpectedly. A crisis struck the campus — a chemical spill in one of the science labs, posing a grave danger to students and staff. The accident caused a chaotic evacuation, with emergency services rushing to contain the situation.

Maaya, sensing the urgency, knew she had to act. Slipping away unnoticed, she used her abilities to assist from the shadows. She manipulated the energies to contain the spread of the chemicals, her actions unseen but crucial in averting a greater disaster.

The incident was a turning point for Maaya. It forced her to confront the reality of her role as a guardian. Her intervention had saved lives, but it had also brought her closer to the truth she had been avoiding – her life would never be normal again. The responsibilities of being a guardian were hers to bear, and they came with sacrifices.

In the aftermath of the crisis, as the university community healed, Maaya found herself being hailed as a hero, her actions on the basketball court a symbol of strength and resilience. Yet, the accolades felt hollow. The real heroism, the one that had truly made a difference, remained hidden, known only to her.

As Maaya walked through the campus, now familiar with its hidden dangers and unseen energies, she realized that her journey was more than just a personal challenge. It was a testament to the courage and resilience of those who walk the fine line between the ordinary and the extraordinary.

Lying in bed at night, Maaya contemplated her future. She had embraced her role as a guardian, but at what cost? The path ahead was uncertain, filled with shadows and light. But Maaya knew one thing for sure – she would walk it with courage, guided by the values that had shaped her, both as Maaya Lakshmi, the university student, and as a guardian of the unseen world.

Chapter 16: Trials of the Guardian

As the spring semester at the University of Lucknow blossomed into full swing, Maaya faced new challenges that tested the limits of her abilities as a guardian. The campus, alive with the energy of student activities and academic pursuits, became a backdrop for Maaya's continued vigilance.

Maaya's nightly patrols, once a source of solitude and reflection, now brought her face-to-face with increasingly complex situations. One night, she encountered a group of students caught in the midst of a heated argument that threatened to escalate into violence. Using her subtle influence, Maaya calmed the tensions, redirecting the students' energies towards a peaceful resolution. It was a small intervention, but one that reaffirmed her role as a protector of harmony.

Another challenge presented itself in a more personal form. A close friend from her basketball team confided in Maaya about a troubling situation involving a family crisis. Maaya, feeling the weight of her friend's distress, used her empathetic abilities to provide comfort and guidance, helping her friend navigate the emotional turmoil. This experience underscored the emotional aspect of her guardianship, extending her role beyond physical interventions to emotional support.

The most significant test, however, came unexpectedly. The university's annual science fair, a showcase of student innovation and research, was disrupted by a dangerous accident. A chemical experiment went awry, causing a panic among the attendees. Maaya, present at the event, sprang into action. Blending into the crowd, she used her powers to contain the chemical reaction, preventing a potential disaster.

This incident was a stark reminder of the unpredictable nature of her role as a guardian. The risks were real, and the impact of her actions far-reaching. Maaya realized that her interventions, though crucial, needed to be carefully executed to avoid unintended consequences.

As the semester progressed, the duality of Maaya's life became even more pronounced. On the basketball court and in her academic endeavours, she excelled, her guardian experiences enhancing her focus and determination. Yet, the secrecy of her double life continued to be a source of inner conflict, a barrier between her and those she cared about.

Maaya's friendship with Priya, in particular, was put to the test. Priya, sensing the changes in Maaya, expressed her concerns about Maaya's well-being. Maaya, torn between her loyalty to her friend and the need to protect her secret, found herself withdrawing further, adding strain to their relationship.

In her quieter moments, Maaya reflected on the trials she had faced. Each challenge had been a learning experience, shaping her into a more adept guardian. Yet, the journey was taking its toll. The balance between her two worlds was becoming increasingly difficult to maintain.

As Maaya lay in bed one night, pondering her path, she realized that the trials of a guardian were not just about-facing external challenges but also about confronting internal struggles. The journey was as much about self-discovery as it was about protecting others.
Determined to continue her role as a guardian while maintaining her personal connections, Maaya resolved to find a way to balance her dual identities. It was a daunting task, but one she was ready to embrace. The trials had strengthened her, and she knew that whatever lay ahead, she would face it with the same courage and

determination that had brought her this far.

Chapter 17: The Mentor

As summer approached, bringing with it the end of the academic year, Maaya Lakshmi found herself at a crossroads. The challenges she had faced as a guardian had shaped her, but they had also left her with questions about the extent of her abilities and the best way to fulfil her responsibilities.

It was during one of her nightly patrols, a time she used for reflection and vigilance, that Maaya encountered a figure who would significantly alter her understanding of her role as a guardian. This person, cloaked in the shadows of a moonlit night, approached Maaya with an air of knowing and purpose.

"You have been doing well, Maaya," the figure spoke, their voice resonant with wisdom. "But the path of a guardian is fraught with complexities that require guidance."

Maaya was initially wary, but there was something about the stranger that piqued her curiosity. "Who are you?" she asked, her guard still up.

"I am someone who has walked the path you're on," the stranger replied, stepping into the moonlight. The figure was an older woman, her eyes reflecting experience and understanding. "I was once a guardian, like you. Now, I seek to guide those who have taken up the mantle."

The woman, introducing herself as Anaya, explained that she had been watching Maaya, impressed by her courage and her intuitive understanding of her role. Anaya offered to mentor Maaya, to help her refine her abilities and navigate the challenges of being a guardian.

Maaya, feeling a mix of relief and excitement, accepted. The prospect of learning from someone who had walked the same path was invaluable. Anaya's mentorship brought new insights into the nature of Maaya's powers and the responsibilities they entailed.

Under Anaya's guidance, Maaya learned to better control her abilities, to use them more effectively and efficiently. Anaya taught her the importance of understanding the flow of natural energies and how to intervene without disrupting the balance.

Their sessions, often held in the quiet corners of the campus or in the serenity of the night, were a blend of practical lessons and philosophical discussions. Anaya shared stories of her time as a guardian, the challenges she faced, and the lessons she learned.

One of the most crucial lessons Anaya imparted was the understanding that a guardian's role was not to solve every problem but to act as a facilitator of balance. "Your power is a tool, not a solution. Use it to empower, to guide, but remember that the course of life must take its natural flow," Anaya advised.

As their time together progressed, Maaya found a newfound confidence in her role as a guardian. The loneliness of her journey was eased by Anaya's presence, her mentorship a beacon in the often-challenging path Maaya tread.

However, Anaya also cautioned Maaya about the dangers that guardians faced. "There are forces that seek to disrupt the balance, to use the energies for their gain. You must be prepared to face them, Maaya," she warned.

As the summer semester drew to a close, Maaya felt a transformation within herself. She was no longer the uncertain guardian trying to understand her role. She had grown, under

Anaya's mentorship, into a protector more confident in her abilities and her purpose.

The bond between Maaya and Anaya grew stronger, a connection forged in the shared experience of their unique roles. Maaya knew that the road ahead would be challenging, but with Anaya's guidance, she was ready to face whatever lay ahead.

Chapter 18: Training and Growth

Under the guidance of her mentor, Anaya, Maaya began a rigorous journey of self-improvement and mastery over her guardian abilities. Anaya's training sessions were not just about enhancing Maaya's control over her powers, but also about understanding the deeper philosophy of being a guardian. Each lesson was a blend of practical skills and wisdom, aimed at preparing Maaya for the complexities of the role she had embraced.

The training took place in various locations around Lucknow, often under the cover of night. Anaya introduced Maaya to advanced techniques of energy manipulation, teaching her how to channel her powers more effectively and with greater precision. She learned to attune herself to the natural flow of energies around her, sensing imbalances and learning how to correct them without causing disruption.

One of the most significant aspects of the training was mastering the art of healing. Anaya showed Maaya how to extend her powers to not only heal minor physical injuries but also to soothe emotional traumas. This aspect of her training deeply resonated with Maaya, as it aligned with her inherent compassion and desire to help others.

Anaya also focused on enhancing Maaya's physical and mental endurance. She taught her how to maintain her energy levels, to remain vigilant and ready in the face of prolonged challenges. They practiced meditation and mindfulness, techniques that helped Maaya achieve a state of inner balance, crucial for a guardian.

As her training progressed, Maaya began to notice a significant improvement in her abilities. She felt more in control, more attuned to her role as a guardian. The doubts and fears that had once clouded her mind were slowly being replaced by a sense of purpose and confidence.

The basketball court continued to be an outlet for Maaya, where she could blend in and enjoy the simpler aspects of her life. Her enhanced abilities, honed through training with Anaya, subtly improved her performance. Her teammates noticed the change, often commenting on her heightened instincts and impeccable timing. Maaya smiled at these observations, knowing they were the by-products of her rigorous training as a guardian.

However, with growth came new challenges. Maaya found it increasingly difficult to balance her university life with her responsibilities as a guardian. Her academic workload, basketball commitments, and training with Anaya often left her exhausted, both physically and mentally.

Priya, ever observant, noticed the toll the hectic schedule was taking on Maaya. "You're pushing yourself too hard," she would say, concern evident in her voice. Maaya appreciated her friend's concern but knew that she couldn't afford to slow down. The role of a guardian was a commitment that demanded everything she had.

As the semester drew to a close, Maaya felt a sense of accomplishment. She had grown not just in terms of her abilities but also in her understanding of what it meant to be a guardian. Anaya's mentorship had been invaluable, providing her with the tools and knowledge she needed to navigate the path ahead.
But Maaya also knew that this was just the beginning. The true test of her abilities and her resolve as a guardian was yet to come. The world beyond the university walls was vast and unpredictable, and Maaya was aware that greater challenges lay ahead.

Armed with her training and guided by her mentor's wisdom, Maaya Lakshmi was ready to face the future, to embrace the full extent of her role as a protector of balance and a guardian of the unseen.

Chapter 19: The Shadow Looms

With the onset of the monsoon season, the University of Lucknow campus transformed into a canvas of lush greens and overcast skies. For Maaya, each raindrop seemed to echo the rhythm of her dual life. The progress she had made under Anaya's mentorship was significant, but as she grew stronger and more adept in her abilities, a sense of foreboding began to take root. Unbeknownst to her, darker forces were stirring, drawn by the ripples of her actions as a guardian.

One humid evening, as Maaya walked through the rain-soaked pathways of the campus, she felt an unfamiliar chill that cut through the warm air. It was a sensation that set her guardian instincts on high alert. Her training had heightened her sensitivity to disruptions in natural energies, and this felt like a harbinger of something ominous.

In the days that followed, Maaya noticed subtle changes around the campus. Unexplainable occurrences, minor yet strange, began to take place – unseasonal weather patterns, disturbances in wildlife behaviour, and an undercurrent of unease among the students and faculty.

Anaya, sensing the shift in energies, confirmed Maaya's suspicions. "There are forces that seek to disrupt the balance we protect," Anaya warned during one of their training sessions. "Your growth as a guardian has not gone unnoticed. You must be prepared for the challenges ahead."

The threat remained vague and shadowy, but its presence was increasingly palpable. Maaya found herself spending more nights patrolling the campus and its surroundings, vigilant for any signs of the lurking danger.

Her commitment to her role as a guardian deepened, but so did the complexity of her life. Balancing her academics, basketball commitments, and guardian responsibilities became a gruelling routine. Priya and her other friends noticed her growing fatigue and preoccupation, mistaking it for academic stress.

The true test came one night when Maaya encountered what she had been sensing all along. In the quiet of the university's botanical garden, she faced a manifestation of the disruptive forces – an entity that seemed to be a distortion of natural energies, its presence an affront to the balance Maaya was sworn to protect.

The encounter was brief but intense. Maaya, relying on her training, managed to dispel the entity, restoring calm to the area. But the encounter left her shaken. It was a clear sign that her role as a guardian would involve confrontations with entities that sought to upset the natural order.

In the aftermath, Maaya and Anaya met to discuss the implications of the encounter. "You have faced your first true test as a guardian," Anaya said solemnly. "But this is just the beginning. Entities like the one you encountered are often pawns in a larger game. We must remain vigilant and prepared."

Maaya understood the gravity of the situation. The shadow that loomed was not just a threat to her but to the equilibrium she had vowed to protect. The battle she had fought in the botanical garden was a small skirmish in what promised to be a larger war against forces that she was only beginning to comprehend.
As Maaya walked back to her dormitory under the starless night sky, her resolve solidified. She was no longer just a student at the University of Lucknow; she was a guardian, a protector against the shadows that threatened the delicate balance of the world. The path ahead was fraught with uncertainty and danger, but

Maaya was ready to face it, armed with her powers, her training, and an unwavering sense of duty.

Chapter 20: Confronting Darkness

In the wake of her first encounter with a malevolent entity, Maaya's role as a guardian took on a new urgency. The University of Lucknow, once a place of academic pursuit and youthful exuberance, now also served as a battleground for unseen forces. Maaya found herself constantly on edge, her senses attuned to any sign of the lurking darkness she had faced.

Under Anaya's guidance, Maaya began preparing for the inevitable confrontations that lay ahead. Their training sessions became more intense, focusing not just on harnessing Maaya's powers, but also on strategy and tactics for dealing with malevolent entities. Anaya emphasized the importance of understanding her adversaries, of anticipating their moves and countering them effectively.

As Maaya honed her skills, the university became rife with rumours and whispers. Stories of strange occurrences and Maaya's late-night wanderings fuelled speculation among the students. Priya, increasingly concerned about her friend's well-being, confronted Maaya. The strain in Maaya's eyes and her evasive answers only deepened Priya's worry.

Meanwhile, the malevolent forces that Maaya had sensed began to manifest more boldly. A series of unexplained incidents around the campus – disturbances in the natural environment, a pervasive sense of unease – escalated into a palpable threat. It became clear that whatever Maaya had faced in the botanical garden was merely a precursor to a more significant danger. The confrontation came on a night of tempestuous weather. As thunder rumbled and lightning illuminated the sky, Maaya felt a surge of discordant energy emanating from the heart of the campus. Guided by her instincts, she raced towards the source of the disturbance.

There, in the midst of the university's central quad, Maaya came face to face with the essence of the darkness she had been sensing. It was a formidable entity, its presence a maelstrom of chaotic energy. The air around it crackled with power, the ground beneath it scarred by its malevolence.

Maaya, drawing upon all her training and strength, confronted the entity. The battle was fierce, a clash of wills and powers. Maaya's every move was a blend of precision and force, her abilities pushed to their limits. The entity, for its part, was relentless, its attacks a barrage of dark energy.

The struggle seemed endless, a test of endurance and resolve. But Maaya, fuelled by her commitment to her duty as a guardian, found an inner reserve of strength. Channelling her powers with focused intent, she managed to weaken the entity, breaking its hold on the area.

As the entity dissipated, the night returned to calm. The quad, once a scene of chaos, was now still, the only evidence of the battle the scorched earth where Maaya had stood her ground.

Exhausted but victorious, Maaya realized the significance of what she had achieved. She had not only protected the university but had also affirmed her role as a guardian. The battle was a testament to her growth and the effectiveness of her training with Anaya.

However, the victory was not without its consequences. The intensity of the confrontation had not gone unnoticed. The next day, the university was abuzz with talk about the strange storm and the mysterious figure seen battling an unseen force.

Maaya knew that her actions had potentially exposed her secret. She also understood that the entity she had defeated was likely a harbinger of more significant challenges to come. The darkness she had confronted was part of a larger, more sinister threat.

As Maaya pondered her next steps, she realized that her journey as a guardian was evolving. She was no longer just reacting to threats; she was actively engaging in a conflict that spanned beyond the boundaries of her university life. The path ahead was daunting, but Maaya was determined to face it, armed with her powers, her training, and an unwavering commitment to her duty as a protector of balance.

Chapter 21: Echoes of Destiny

The aftermath of Maaya's confrontation with the dark entity brought a new reality to her life as a guardian. The University of Lucknow, once a haven of academic pursuits and youthful dreams, now bore the marks of her secret battle. While the physical scars were subtle, the psychic impact was profound, both on Maaya and on the campus community.

In the days following the battle, Maaya wrestled with the implications of her actions. She had successfully protected the university, but the visibility of her confrontation raised concerns about her anonymity as a guardian. Whispers and rumours circulated among the students and faculty, fuelling a mix of awe and apprehension.

Priya, who had grown increasingly worried about Maaya, confronted her again. This time, her questions were more pointed, driven by the strange occurrences and the rumours of a mysterious figure during the night of the storm. Maaya, caught between her duty as a guardian and her loyalty to her friend, found herself at a crossroads. The burden of her secret had never felt heavier.

Meanwhile, Anaya provided counsel and support. She reminded Maaya of the guardian's path, one that was often solitary and fraught with difficult choices. "Your journey is not just about confronting darkness," Anaya said. "It's also about understanding the deeper connections of your actions, the ripples they create in the world around you."

Reflecting on Anaya's words, Maaya began to see her role in a broader context. She realized that her destiny as a guardian was intricately linked to the fabric of life around her. Her actions, while necessary, had consequences that extended beyond the immediate moments of confrontation.

This realization was further deepened when Maaya discovered that the energy disturbances caused by her battle had subtly affected the natural balance of the campus. She spent several nights restoring the equilibrium, her powers working gently to heal the unseen wounds inflicted on the environment.

As she engaged in this restorative process, Maaya felt a profound connection to her role. She understood that being a guardian was not just about battling threats, but also about nurturing and preserving the harmony of the world she was sworn to protect.

The echoes of her destiny resounded beyond the physical realm, touching the lives of those around her. Maaya's professors noticed a change in her demeanour, a newfound depth in her academic work. Her basketball coach commented on her heightened focus and leadership on the court. And in her quiet moments with Priya, despite the unspoken secrets, there was an unbreakable bond of friendship and trust.

Maaya's journey as a guardian had become an integral part of her identity, shaping her interactions and her view of the world. It was a path that required sacrifice and resilience, but it was also a path of profound growth and fulfilment.

As the semester drew to a close, Maaya stood at a pivotal point in her journey. She had faced the shadows, embraced her destiny, and emerged stronger. The road ahead promised new challenges and revelations, but Maaya was ready to face them with the wisdom of her experiences and the strength of her resolve.

Chapter 22: Alliance of Light

As summer deepened at the University of Lucknow, Maaya found herself reflecting on the journey she had embarked upon. The campus, with its vibrant student life and verdant surroundings, continued to be a backdrop to her dual existence. However, recent events had brought a new clarity to Maaya's role as a guardian. She understood that the challenges ahead required not just strength and skill, but also alliances and cooperation.

This realization was solidified when Maaya encountered Aarav, a fellow student with an interest in environmental activism. Aarav's passion for nature and his intuitive understanding of ecological balance intrigued Maaya. Their conversations often delved into topics of natural harmony and the unseen forces that govern it.

As they spent more time together, Maaya sensed a kinship with Aarav, a shared understanding of the world's delicate balance. She began to wonder if he, like her, had a deeper connection to the natural world. The idea of finding someone who shared her understanding of the guardian's path was both exciting and nerve-wracking.

Meanwhile, Anaya continued to guide Maaya, offering wisdom and support. During one of their training sessions, Maaya broached the subject of alliances. Anaya's response was thoughtful. "Being a guardian often requires solitude, but it does not mean you must walk the path alone. Allies who share your vision and values can be a great strength," she advised.

Encouraged by Anaya's words, Maaya decided to cautiously explore the possibility of an alliance with Aarav. One evening, under the guise of discussing a university project, Maaya steered their conversation towards the topic of guardianship and the balance of nature.

To her surprise and relief, Aarav responded with keen interest. He shared his observations of the subtle changes in the campus environment and his theories about the existence of energies beyond the ordinary. Maaya listened, a growing sense of hope and excitement building within her.

As their discussions progressed, Maaya felt a deepening trust in Aarav. She contemplated revealing her identity as a guardian to him, to forge an alliance based on mutual understanding and shared purpose.

The opportunity presented itself when the campus faced an environmental crisis. A sudden infestation of invasive plant species threatened the local ecosystem, causing disruptions in the campus's natural balance. Maaya and Aarav worked together, combining their knowledge and efforts to address the issue.

In the midst of this collaboration, Maaya took a leap of faith. She revealed her powers to Aarav, demonstrating her ability to manipulate natural energies to restore balance. Aarav, amazed by the revelation, accepted the truth with an open mind and heart.

The alliance between Maaya and Aarav marked a turning point in Maaya's journey. Aarav's insights and his understanding of ecological dynamics complemented Maaya's guardian abilities. Together, they formed a bond of mutual respect and cooperation, an alliance of light against the challenges they faced.

As the summer semester drew to a close, Maaya looked back at the progress she had made. Her alliance with Aarav, her growing mastery of her powers under Anaya's mentorship, and her deeper understanding of her role as a guardian had prepared her for the path ahead.

Maaya stood ready to face the future, not just as a solitary guardian but as part of a collective effort to protect and preserve the balance of the natural world. The journey ahead was uncertain, but Maaya was no longer alone. She had allies by her side, and together, they would face whatever challenges lay ahead in the journey of light and guardianship.

Chapter 23: A Greater Purpose

As the monsoon season gave way to clear skies, Maaya felt a shift within herself. The alliance with Aarav had opened new avenues in her role as a guardian. Working together, they had begun to address not just immediate threats but also broader environmental issues affecting the University of Lucknow and its surroundings.

This period of collaboration and shared purpose brought a new perspective to Maaya's understanding of her guardianship. It wasn't just about reacting to disturbances or threats; it was also about proactive stewardship of the natural world. Aarav's knowledge of environmental science complemented Maaya's abilities, allowing them to implement changes that fostered harmony and balance.

Anaya observed this evolution in Maaya with pride. "You are understanding the true essence of being a guardian, Maaya," she said during one of their sessions. "It is about seeing the larger picture, about realizing that every action we take as guardians impacts the world in ways both seen and unseen."

Encouraged by Anaya's words, Maaya began to embrace a broader vision of her role. She started to engage more with campus initiatives focused on sustainability and conservation, using her influence and knowledge to steer projects and discussions. Her actions, though subtle, began to create a positive ripple effect throughout the university community.

However, with this expanded scope of activity came new challenges. Balancing her academic responsibilities, her role on the basketball team, and her guardianship duties became increasingly demanding. Maaya found herself stretched thin, her time and energy constantly divided among her various commitments.

Priya, who had been a pillar of support despite the secrets between them, noticed the strain on Maaya. "You're trying to do too much, Maaya," she cautioned. "Remember, you don't have to carry every burden alone." Her words echoed in Maaya's mind, a reminder of the importance of balance and self-care.

Meanwhile, the greater purpose Maaya had embraced began to draw attention beyond the university. Other students, inspired by the changes they saw, started to take an active interest in environmental and sustainability issues. Maaya's leadership, though quiet and unassuming, was inspiring a movement of awareness and action.

The turning point came when the university announced a major project to create a green corridor within the campus, a space dedicated to biodiversity and environmental education. Maaya and Aarav were at the forefront of this initiative, their alliance proving to be a powerful force for positive change.

As Maaya worked on the project, she realized that her journey as a guardian had taken on a new dimension. It was no longer just about protecting against threats; it was about being a catalyst for change, about inspiring others to see the interconnectedness of all life and the importance of living in harmony with nature.

This realization was empowering but also humbling. Maaya understood that her role as a guardian was part of a larger tapestry, one that involved many threads and colours. She was but one piece in the puzzle of guardianship, contributing to a purpose that spanned beyond her individual actions.

As the green corridor project neared completion, Maaya looked back on her journey with a sense of fulfilment and anticipation. She had grown, not just in her abilities as a guardian but in her understanding of what it truly meant to serve a greater purpose. The road ahead was filled with possibilities and challenges, but Maaya was ready to meet them, guided by her commitment to protect and preserve the balance of the natural world.

Chapter 24: Challenges of the Protector

The completion of the green corridor project at the University of Lucknow marked a significant achievement for Maaya and Aarav. It stood as a testament to their collaborative effort and Maaya's growing influence as a guardian. However, the success of the project also brought new challenges to Maaya's life, both as a university student and as a protector of balance.

With the increasing visibility of her environmental initiatives, Maaya found herself in the spotlight more than she was comfortable with. Her efforts on the green corridor project had garnered attention from the university administration and her peers, leading to an expectation for her to lead similar initiatives. Balancing these expectations with her academic responsibilities and her secret life as a guardian became increasingly difficult.

Moreover, the success of the green corridor project had an unintended consequence. It drew the attention of external parties interested in the university's environmental efforts. While most were well-intentioned, some saw it as an opportunity for their gain, threatening the delicate balance Maaya had worked so hard to maintain.

One such challenge emerged when a local business consortium proposed a partnership with the university to expand the green corridor into a larger commercial project. The proposal, while promising significant funding and resources, strayed from the project's original purpose of conservation and education.

Maaya, sensing the potential disruption this partnership could cause to the natural balance, found herself at odds with university officials and some faculty members who supported the proposal.

Her attempts to voice her concerns were met with resistance, and for the first time, Maaya felt the limitations of her influence as a student.

In the midst of this turmoil, Maaya continued her nightly duties as a guardian. The balance she strove to protect extended beyond the university campus, and her responsibilities often took her to the city's outskirts. Here, she encountered different challenges – environmental degradation, disturbances in natural habitats, and occasional encounters with malevolent entities drawn to the city's growing imbalance.

These nightly excursions were a stark reminder of the broader scope of her role as a guardian. The university's issues were but a microcosm of the larger challenges facing the natural world. Maaya realized that her actions, however impactful at the university, were part of a much larger fight to maintain harmony and balance.

Anaya, ever the wise mentor, provided guidance and support during these challenging times. "Remember, Maaya, the path of a guardian is fraught with obstacles. But each challenge is an opportunity to grow, to reaffirm your commitment to your role," she advised.

As the debate over the green corridor project continued, Maaya found an ally in Priya. Despite not knowing Maaya's secret, Priya stood by her friend, supporting her efforts to maintain the project's integrity. This support was a source of strength for Maaya, a reminder that her journey as a guardian did not mean she was alone.

The challenges Maaya faced as a protector were a constant test of her resolve and her abilities. Each decision, each action, had to be weighed against the potential impact on the balance she was sworn to protect. It was a burden she carried with a sense of duty and determination.

As the semester drew to a close, Maaya reflected on her journey. The challenges she faced had shaped her, not just as a guardian but as an individual. She had learned the importance of resilience, of standing firm in her beliefs, and of the strength found in alliances. The road ahead was uncertain, filled with both opportunities and obstacles, but Maaya was ready to face them, armed with her powers, her experiences, and the support of those who believed in her.

Chapter 25: The Warrior's Path

As the academic year at the University of Lucknow drew to a close, Maaya found herself at a pivotal juncture in her journey as a guardian. The challenges she had faced, both on campus with the green corridor project and beyond in her role as a protector, had forged her into a more resilient and determined figure. However, the path ahead promised even greater trials.

Maaya's success in maintaining the integrity of the green corridor project against commercial interests had established her as a key environmental advocate on campus. While this recognition brought her a sense of accomplishment, it also placed her in the spotlight, a position she had always sought to avoid.

The heightened visibility brought new challenges. Maaya found herself navigating a complex web of university politics and external pressures. Each decision she made, each stance she took, had repercussions that rippled beyond her immediate circle.

In the midst of these challenges, Maaya continued her nightly patrols as a guardian. The city of Lucknow, with its blend of ancient heritage and modern growth, was a landscape filled with energies that required constant vigilance. Maaya's encounters with malevolent entities grew more frequent, a sign that the balance she sought to protect was under increasing threat.

During one such patrol, Maaya faced an entity more powerful than any she had encountered before. The battle that ensued tested the limits of her abilities and her endurance. It was a stark reminder that her role as a guardian involved not just protecting the natural balance but also combating forces that sought to disrupt it.

The experience was a turning point for Maaya. She realized that her journey as a guardian was akin to walking a warrior's path. It required not just physical strength and powers but also mental fortitude and strategic thinking. The battles she fought were not just against external entities but also against the doubts and fears within her.

Anaya, sensing the shift in Maaya's perspective, offered guidance. "The path of a warrior is not chosen lightly," she said. "It demands everything of you – your strength, your wisdom, and your heart. Remember, Maaya, that the true strength of a warrior lies not in their ability to wage war, but in their ability to maintain peace."

These words resonated with Maaya. She understood that her actions as a guardian had broader implications, that her battles were part of a larger struggle to maintain harmony in a world where the lines between natural and supernatural were increasingly blurred.

As Maaya prepared to leave the university for the summer break, she reflected on her journey. She had evolved from a student and an athlete into a guardian and a warrior. The experiences she had gained, the challenges she had overcome, and the alliances she had formed had prepared her for the next phase of her journey.

The warrior's path was a solitary one, but Maaya was not alone. She had allies like Aarav and Priya, and a mentor in Anaya. Their support and belief in her gave her strength.

Maaya left the university with a sense of purpose and determination. The summer promised a respite from academic responsibilities, but for Maaya, the role of a guardian never paused. She was ready to continue her journey, to walk the warrior's path with courage and resolve, protecting the balance of the world against the shadows that threatened it.

Chapter 26: The First Victory

With the university closed for the summer, the streets of Lucknow took on a quieter, more languid character. For Maaya, however, the change of pace brought no respite. Her role as a guardian led her deeper into the heart of the city, where the balance between the natural and supernatural realms felt increasingly precarious.

The city's rich tapestry of history and modernity provided a backdrop for a series of encounters that tested Maaya's abilities and resolve. Each confrontation with malevolent entities, each intervention to restore balance, honed her skills and deepened her understanding of her role as a guardian.

It was during one of these encounters that Maaya faced a challenge unlike any before. A powerful entity, drawn to the city's growing imbalance, began to wreak havoc in one of the oldest parts of Lucknow. Its presence disturbed the natural order, causing environmental anomalies and instilling fear among the residents.

Maaya, sensing the urgency of the situation, embarked on a mission to confront and neutralize the entity. This battle was more than a test of her powers; it was a fight to protect the city she had come to cherish, a city that was an integral part of her own journey.

The confrontation was intense and demanding. Maaya found herself pushed to her limits, employing every skill she had learned from Anaya and drawing on the inner strength she had cultivated. The entity was formidable, its power rooted in the very disturbances Maaya sought to heal.

As the battle raged, Maaya's resolve never wavered. She maneuverer with agility and precision, countering the entity's attacks with strategic use of her abilities. The fight was a dance of power and skill, a testament to Maaya's growth as a guardian.

In the end, it was Maaya's deep connection to the natural order, her understanding of the balance she was sworn to protect, that turned the tide. Channelling her energies, she managed to weaken the entity, ultimately dispersing its presence and restoring calm to the area.

The victory was a significant milestone for Maaya. It marked her first major triumph in the broader battle to maintain harmony in the face of growing threats. The citizens of Lucknow remained unaware of the guardian who had protected them, but Maaya felt a deep sense of accomplishment and purpose.

In the aftermath of the battle, as Maaya walked through the now-peaceful streets of the old city, she reflected on her journey. She had come a long way from the uncertain, reluctant guardian she had once been. The challenges she had faced had shaped her into a warrior for balance, a defender against the forces that sought to disrupt the natural order.

This first victory was more than just a personal triumph; it was a validation of her path as a guardian. Maaya knew that there would be more challenges ahead, that her journey was far from over. But she also knew that she was ready to face whatever lay ahead, armed with her powers, her training, and a newfound confidence in her role as a protector.

As the summer stars twinkled above the city of Lucknow, Maaya felt a connection to something greater than herself, a sense of being part of a timeless struggle to maintain the harmony of the world. She was Maaya Lakshmi, a student, a basketball player, and now, a proven guardian of balance.

Chapter 27: Reflections and Revelations

The victory over the powerful entity in the heart of Lucknow marked a significant milestone in Maaya's journey as a guardian. As the summer progressed, Maaya found herself in a reflective state, pondering the path she had walked and the future that lay ahead.

This period of introspection was further deepened by a series of revelations that reshaped her understanding of her role. Anaya, sensing Maaya's readiness for deeper knowledge, shared insights into the history and lore of guardians. She spoke of the ancient lineage to which Maaya belonged, a lineage that traced back centuries, each guardian tasked with maintaining the balance between the natural and supernatural realms.

These revelations were both awe-inspiring and daunting. Maaya learned that her battles were part of a larger cosmic struggle, a struggle that guardians through the ages had engaged in. The knowledge of her place in this lineage brought a sense of pride but also a weightier sense of responsibility.

During this time, Maaya also deepened her bond with Aarav. Their shared commitment to environmental balance and sustainability had blossomed into a strong partnership. Aarav, while not privy to the full extent of Maaya's guardian role, provided support and insight that proved invaluable in Maaya's endeavours.

This period was also one of personal growth for Maaya. She began to see her powers not just as tools for battle, but as means of fostering harmony and understanding. She used her abilities to heal and nurture, to connect more deeply with the natural world, and to guide others towards a path of sustainability and respect for nature.

However, the revelations also brought new challenges. Maaya understood that the entity she had defeated was likely a precursor to greater threats. The balance she was sworn to protect was fragile, and there were forces at work that sought to tip it into chaos.

Maaya's reflections during this time led her to a deeper realization about her identity. She was more than a student, more than a basketball player, and more than a guardian. She was a synthesis of all these roles, each aspect integral to her being. This understanding brought a newfound sense of wholeness and purpose.

As the summer drew to a close and the university prepared to welcome students back, Maaya felt a renewed sense of resolve. The path of a guardian was complex and fraught with challenges, but it was also filled with opportunities for growth and positive impact.

Maaya returned to the University of Lucknow with a clearer vision of her role. She was ready to face the challenges ahead, armed with the knowledge of her lineage, the strength of her alliances, and the depth of her experiences.

The journey ahead promised new battles and trials, but also the chance to forge a better future, to protect the delicate balance that sustained life in all its forms. Maaya Lakshmi, a guardian of ancient lineage, stood ready to uphold her duty, to be a beacon of light in a world that teetered on the edge of shadow and light.

Chapter 28: Gathering Storm

As the new academic year began at the University of Lucknow, a sense of anticipation hung in the air, mixed with the familiar buzz of student activities. For Maaya, returning to the university was a return to a battlefield of sorts, where her dual roles as a student and a guardian continued to intertwine.

The revelations of the summer had given Maaya a new perspective on her role as a guardian. She understood that the skirmishes she had engaged in were part of a larger conflict, a gathering storm that threatened the delicate balance she was sworn to protect.

This realization was brought into sharp focus when a series of unusual environmental phenomena began to occur around Lucknow. Unseasonal weather patterns, disturbances in wildlife behaviour, and a general sense of unease pervaded the city. These anomalies were not just random occurrences; they were symptomatic of a deeper imbalance.

Maaya, with her heightened sensitivity to the natural order, felt the undercurrents of this growing storm. She knew that the forces she had been contending with were gaining strength, converging towards a point of crisis.

The situation was compounded by the arrival of a new figure on campus, a visiting scholar named Dr. Vikram Singh. Dr. Singh, an expert in environmental science, brought with him theories and practices that challenged the conventional understanding of nature and its forces. His charismatic presence and radical ideas quickly garnered a following among the students and faculty.

Maaya, intrigued by Dr. Singh's arrival, attended his lectures. She found his views compelling but also unsettling. There was something about Dr. Singh that resonated with the disturbances she had been sensing. Her guardian instincts told her to be wary, to probe deeper into Dr. Singh's true intentions.

Meanwhile, Maaya continued to strengthen her alliance with Aarav, working together on environmental initiatives on campus. Aarav's support and insight were invaluable, but Maaya was careful not to involve him too deeply in her guardian responsibilities, aware of the dangers it posed.

Her mentor, Anaya, provided guidance during this tumultuous time. "The gathering storm you sense is a convergence of energies, both natural and supernatural," Anaya explained. "You must be prepared for what is to come. The balance you strive to maintain will be tested like never before."

As the semester progressed, the signs of the approaching storm became more apparent. Maaya found herself dealing with increasing incidents of environmental and supernatural disturbances. Each encounter, each intervention, was a preparation for the larger conflict that loomed.

Maaya's nights were spent patrolling the city, her days immersed in academic and environmental work. The dual aspects of her life were more demanding than ever, but Maaya faced each challenge with determination. She knew that the role of a guardian was not just about battling threats but also about being a custodian of harmony.

The climax of this growing conflict came one fateful night when a massive disturbance in the city's energies brought Maaya face to face with the true nature of the gathering storm. The confrontation that ensued tested all that Maaya had learned, pushing her to the brink of her abilities.

As dawn broke over the city of Lucknow, the aftermath of the night's events left Maaya with a deeper understanding of the challenges ahead. The storm she had sensed was just beginning to unfold, and she was at the heart of it. The path of a guardian was a path of constant vigilance and courage, and Maaya was ready to walk it, no matter the cost.

Chapter 29: The Battle Begins

As the academic year at the University of Lucknow progressed, the sense of an impending storm Maaya had felt became increasingly tangible. The city, steeped in history and tradition, seemed to be at the epicentre of a brewing conflict that blurred the lines between the natural and the supernatural.

Dr. Vikram Singh's presence on campus had become a catalyst for change. His ideas, though radical, resonated with many, creating a divide among the students and faculty. Maaya observed his influence with caution, sensing an undercurrent of energy around him that was unsettling.

It was during a major environmental symposium organized by the university that the latent conflict came to a head. The event, meant to be a platform for discussing sustainable practices, turned into a battleground of ideologies. Dr. Singh's keynote speech, advocating for a new order of interaction with the natural world, was charismatic yet divisive.

Maaya, attending the symposium, felt a surge of discordant energy. Her instincts as a guardian told her that this was more than just a clash of ideas – it was the spark that would ignite the larger battle she had been anticipating.

As Dr. Singh's speech reached its climax, the energy in the room shifted dramatically. The atmosphere became charged, and a sense of unease spread among the attendees. It was then that the true nature of the storm revealed itself.

From the shadows of the auditorium, entities of darkness, drawn by the tumultuous energy, emerged. The crowd panicked, chaos ensued, and the symposium turned into a scene of confusion and fear.

Maaya sprang into action. Drawing upon all her training and powers, she confronted the entities, her every move a blend of precision and force. The battle was fierce, a manifestation of the conflict between the guardians of balance and the forces that sought to disrupt it.

Dr. Singh, witnessing the chaos, revealed his true intentions. He was not just a scholar with radical ideas; he was a manipulator of energies, seeking to harness the forces of nature for his own purposes. His actions had been a deliberate ploy to destabilize the balance, to create a power he could control.

The revelation of Dr. Singh's betrayal added a new layer of complexity to the battle. Maaya realized that the conflict was not just against dark entities but against human ambition that threatened the natural order.

With the help of Aarav, who had joined her in the midst of the chaos, Maaya fought to restore balance. Together, they worked to dispel the entities and counteract the disruptive energies unleashed by Dr. Singh.

The battle raged, a tumultuous clash of powers within the walls of the university. Maaya and Aarav stood their ground, their determination unwavering. Finally, after what seemed like an eternity, the tide turned. The entities were vanquished, and Dr. Singh's plans were thwarted.

The aftermath of the battle left the university community shaken but safe. Dr. Singh's true motives were exposed, and he was taken into custody. The symposium, meant to be a forum for learning and growth, had become the site of a significant victory for Maaya and her allies.

As the dust settled, Maaya reflected on the events. The battle had been a crucial test of her abilities as a guardian. She had faced not just supernatural adversaries but also the darker aspects of human ambition and greed.

The victory was significant, but Maaya knew that it was just one battle in a larger war. The forces that sought to disrupt the balance were still at large, their intentions unknown. The path of a guardian was a constant struggle, but Maaya was resolute. She had emerged from the battle stronger, more determined to protect the harmony of the world she was sworn to defend.

Chapter 30: Trials of Strength and Will

In the aftermath of the tumultuous battle at the environmental symposium, Maaya's role as a guardian took on a new level of intensity. The confrontation with Dr. Vikram Singh and the dark entities had exposed the depth of the threat to the natural balance. It was a stark reminder that her journey as a guardian would be fraught with trials that tested not just her strength but also her will.

The University of Lucknow, still reeling from the events of the symposium, became a hub of heightened activity. Students and faculty alike struggled to make sense of what had happened. Amidst this turmoil, Maaya found herself at the centre of attention, her role in the conflict a subject of much speculation and admiration.

However, the victory at the symposium was not without its costs. Maaya felt the physical and emotional toll of the battle. Her powers, though formidable, had been pushed to their limits. The encounter with Dr. Singh had revealed vulnerabilities she hadn't been fully aware of, and the realization weighed heavily on her.

In the weeks that followed, Maaya faced a series of challenges that tested her resilience. The city of Lucknow, with its blend of ancient history and burgeoning modernity, seemed to be a magnet for disturbances in the natural order. Maaya found herself dealing with a surge in supernatural activity, each incident a test of her abilities as a guardian.

These confrontations were diverse – from calming a sudden, unexplained storm that threatened to flood parts of the city, to countering a wave of negative energy that had inexplicably enveloped a local neighbourhood. Each challenge required Maaya to adapt and strategize, to use her powers in innovative ways.

Amidst these trials, Maaya's relationship with Aarav deepened. His support and understanding provided her with much-needed respite from her responsibilities. Aarav, aware of the full extent of Maaya's role as a guardian, became an invaluable ally, offering his knowledge of environmental science to help predict and mitigate the disturbances they faced.

However, the ongoing trials put a strain on Maaya's other relationships. Priya, her closest friend, felt the growing distance between them. Maaya's secretive and increasingly hectic life made it difficult for her to maintain the close bond they once shared. The strain was evident, and Maaya grappled with the guilt of keeping Priya in the dark.

Anaya, ever the wise mentor, provided guidance during these challenging times. "The path of a guardian is a continuous test of your strength and will," Anaya reminded Maaya. "Each challenge you face is an opportunity to grow, to understand the depth of your powers and the breadth of your responsibility."

As the semester progressed, Maaya's resolve was fortified by the trials she faced. She grew more adept at managing her dual life, finding a balance between her academic responsibilities, her environmental initiatives, and her role as a guardian.

The trials Maaya endured were not just battles against external forces; they were also internal struggles of growth and self-discovery. With each challenge, she learned more about her strengths and weaknesses, about the resilience of her spirit, and the unwavering commitment to her duty as a guardian.

As the university year drew to a close, Maaya looked back on a period of significant growth and challenge. She had emerged from the trials stronger, more determined, and more aware of the crucial role she played in maintaining the balance between the natural and supernatural worlds.

The journey ahead promised more trials, more growth, and more opportunities to prove her strength and will. Maaya was ready to face them, her resolve unshaken, her spirit undeterred.

Chapter 31: Darkness Before Dawn

The end of the academic year at the University of Lucknow was marked by a palpable tension, a reflection of the unseen battles that Maaya had been waging. As a guardian, she had faced numerous trials, each one a testament to her growing strength and resolve. However, the increasing frequency and intensity of these challenges hinted at a looming larger conflict, a darkness before the proverbial dawn.

One night, as Maaya patrolled the city, she felt an overwhelming surge of malevolent energy. It was unlike anything she had encountered before, a dark tide that threatened to engulf Lucknow in chaos. The source of this energy seemed to emanate from the ancient heart of the city, a place steeped in history and legend.

As Maaya navigated the narrow, winding streets, the sense of foreboding grew stronger. She arrived at an old, abandoned temple, the epicentre of the dark energy. Here, she was confronted by a powerful entity, a being that seemed to be a manifestation of the darkness itself.

The entity was formidable, its power rooted in centuries of forgotten lore and hidden malice. Maaya engaged in battle, but quickly realized that she was outmatched. The entity's strength was overwhelming, its attacks a maelstrom of dark energy that threatened to consume her.

In the midst of the battle, Maaya's resolve wavered. The realization that she might not be able to overcome this adversary filled her with doubt and fear. The guardian spirit that had guided her seemed distant, and for the first time, Maaya felt truly alone in her fight.

As the entity bore down on her, Maaya grappled with a sense of despair. The darkness before her was a reflection of her deepest fears – the fear of failure, the fear of not being strong enough to protect the balance she was sworn to uphold.

In that moment of darkness, Maaya's thoughts turned to the people she cared about – her friends at the university, her mentor Anaya, and her ally Aarav. She thought of the city of Lucknow, with its vibrant life and rich history, now threatened by the entity before her. The realization that so much was at stake reignited her spirit.

Drawing upon every reserve of strength and will, Maaya rallied against the entity. She channelled her powers with renewed focus, countering the entity's assaults with a series of strategic moves. The battle was a clash of light and darkness, a struggle for the soul of the city.

After what seemed like an eternity, Maaya found an opening. With a final burst of energy, she managed to weaken the entity, dispersing its dark presence. The temple, once a site of malevolence, was now still, bathed in the soft light of dawn.

Exhausted and shaken, Maaya emerged from the battle victorious but humbled. The confrontation had pushed her to the brink, testing not just her powers, but the very core of her being. It was a stark reminder of the enormity of her role as a guardian and the constant danger that lurked in the shadows.

As the first rays of dawn broke over Lucknow, Maaya reflected on her journey. She had faced the darkness, both within and without, and had emerged stronger. The path of a guardian was fraught with trials, but it was also a path of growth and discovery.

The darkness before dawn had been a crucible, a test of her

strength and will. Maaya had risen to the challenge, reaffirming her commitment to her duty as a guardian. With renewed resolve, she was ready to face whatever the future held, to protect the balance between light and darkness.

Chapter 32: Awakening of True Power

The battle at the old temple had been a defining moment for Maaya. In facing the darkness and overcoming her deepest fears, she experienced an awakening, a realization of the true extent of her powers and her role as a guardian. This experience marked a turning point in her journey, opening her eyes to the possibilities and responsibilities of her abilities.

As Maaya recovered from the battle, she found herself introspective, pondering the lessons she had learned. The confrontation with the powerful entity had pushed her to the edge, but it had also revealed a strength she hadn't fully realized she possessed. It was as if the battle had unlocked a deeper layer of her powers, a connection to the ancient lineage of guardians that flowed through her.

Anaya, recognizing the change in Maaya, guided her through this period of awakening. "You have reached a new stage in your journey," Anaya said. "The power you wield is not just a manifestation of your will; it is a legacy passed down through generations of guardians. You are now tapping into the true essence of that legacy."

Maaya's training with Anaya took on a new dimension. They delved deeper into the ancient lore of the guardians, exploring the mystical aspects of her powers. Maaya learned to channel her energies in ways she had never thought possible, tapping into the natural forces around her with greater ease and precision.

This awakening of her true power also brought a renewed sense of purpose. Maaya realized that her role as a guardian was more significant than she had initially understood. She was not just protecting the balance in Lucknow; she was part of a global network of guardians, each playing a crucial role in maintaining the harmony of the world.

With this realization, Maaya began to approach her duties with a new perspective. She became more proactive in her efforts to sense and prevent disturbances in the natural order. Her interventions became more strategic, guided by a deeper understanding of the interconnectedness of all things.

The awakening of her true power also had a profound impact on her personal life. Maaya found herself more confident and assertive, her interactions with friends and colleagues imbued with a newfound clarity and wisdom. Her relationship with Aarav deepened their partnership strengthened by Maaya's growth and self-assurance.

However, with great power came great responsibility. Maaya knew that her enhanced abilities would attract the attention of those who sought to disrupt the balance. She prepared herself for the challenges ahead, aware that the path of a guardian was never easy.
As the academic year resumed, Maaya returned to the University of Lucknow with a sense of determination. She was more than just a student or a basketball player; she was a guardian with a profound duty to protect the world from the shadows that sought to destabilize it.

The awakening of her true power was both an end and a beginning – the end of her initial uncertainties and fears, and the beginning of a new chapter in her journey as a guardian. Maaya embraced this new chapter with courage and resolve, ready to face whatever the future held.

Chapter 33: The Turning Tide

The awakening of Maaya's true power heralded a new phase in her journey as a guardian. With a deeper understanding of her role and enhanced abilities, she began to address the disturbances in Lucknow's natural balance with a newfound efficacy. The city, with its rich history and vibrant culture, became the canvas upon which she honed her guardianship, subtly weaving harmony into its fabric.

However, the forces that sought to disrupt this balance were ever-present. Maaya's increased activity did not go unnoticed, drawing the attention of entities and individuals who viewed her as a threat to their own chaotic agendas. The city, a microcosm of the larger world, became a battleground for opposing forces of harmony and discord.

One of these forces emerged in the form of a mysterious group that had been influencing the city's energies for their own purposes. Their actions were subtle but insidious, creating ripples of imbalance that Maaya found increasingly challenging to rectify.

The turning tide came when Maaya uncovered the group's plan to destabilize a significant cultural festival in Lucknow. The festival, a celebration of the city's heritage and community spirit, was integral to the city's identity. The group aimed to use this event to amplify negative energies, creating a vortex of disharmony that would have far-reaching consequences.

Armed with this knowledge, Maaya prepared to confront the group. She understood that this was not just a battle of powers, but a fight to preserve the heart and soul of the city. The festival, with its gathering of people and outpouring of positive emotions, was the perfect counter to the group's intentions.

As the festival began, Maaya, with Aarav by her side, moved discreetly among the crowds. Her senses attuned to the flow of energies, she identified and countered the subtle manipulations of the group. It was a delicate task, requiring precision and care to avoid causing alarm among the festivalgoers.

The climax came when Maaya confronted the leader of the group, a figure shrouded in dark energies. The confrontation was intense, a clash of wills that resonated with the power of their opposing intentions. Maaya, drawing upon her connection to the ancient lineage of guardians, channelled her powers to disrupt the leader's influence.

The battle was fierce, but Maaya's resolve was unwavering. With each move, she reclaimed the energies that had been twisted, weaving them back into the tapestry of harmony. The leader, realizing the futility of their efforts against Maaya's newfound strength, retreated, their plans thwarted.

The festival continued, a vibrant celebration of life and community, oblivious to the battle that had taken place in its midst. Maaya, watching over the festivities, felt a profound sense of accomplishment. She had protected not just the physical city but the spirit that animated it.

The turning tide marked a significant victory for Maaya. It was a testament to her growth as a guardian and the efficacy of her powers. She had faced a formidable adversary and emerged victorious, reinforcing her commitment to her role as a protector of balance.

As the festival lights twinkled in the night, reflecting off the waters of the Gomti River, Maaya contemplated her journey. She had faced trials and tribulations, each one shaping her into the guardian she was now. The path ahead would undoubtedly hold more challenges, but Maaya was ready. She had turned the tide once, and she would do it again, standing as a beacon of light against the shadows that sought to encroach upon the world.

Chapter 34: The Protector's Resolve

The successful defence of the cultural festival and the defeat of the shadowy group marked a turning point in Maaya's journey. It was a clear demonstration of her growth as a guardian, her ability to protect not just the physical aspects of Lucknow but also its cultural and spiritual essence. This victory, however, was not just an end; it was the beginning of a new chapter in her guardianship.

In the weeks that followed, Maaya's reputation as a protector of the city's balance grew. Though her actions were often behind the scenes, the effects were felt by many. The city seemed brighter, its energies more harmonious. People began to speak of a guardian spirit watching over Lucknow, a being who ensured the well-being of the city and its inhabitants.

This growing recognition brought Maaya a sense of fulfilment but also a realization of the weight of her responsibilities. She understood that her role as a guardian was an ongoing commitment, one that required constant vigilance and resolve.

The resolve of the protector was tested when a new challenge emerged. A series of natural disturbances began to occur around Lucknow, more intense and frequent than anything Maaya had encountered before. These disturbances were not just random acts of nature; they were symptomatic of a deeper imbalance, a sign of a brewing storm that threatened to engulf the city.

Maaya, with her heightened senses and deep connection to the natural world, sensed that these disturbances were interconnected. They were pieces of a larger puzzle, and she needed to understand the bigger picture to address the root cause of the imbalance.
Her investigation led her to uncover a network of dark energies that had infiltrated the city's ley lines, the pathways of natural

energy that flowed through Lucknow. This network was feeding off the city's energies, creating a vortex of disharmony that manifested in the physical disturbances.

Realizing the magnitude of the threat, Maaya knew she needed to act swiftly. She reached out to Aarav, seeking his help in understanding the environmental impact of these disturbances. Together, they worked to map out the ley lines, identifying the key points where the dark energies were most concentrated.

The task ahead was daunting. Maaya needed to cleanse the ley lines, to restore the natural flow of energies and bring balance back to the city. It was a task that required not just power but also precision and a deep understanding of the intricate web of natural forces.

As Maaya embarked on this mission, she felt the full weight of her role as a guardian. Each step she took, each line she cleansed, brought her closer to restoring harmony. The process was exhausting, both physically and mentally, but Maaya's resolve never faltered.

Her efforts culminated in a night of intense activity. Maaya, channelling her powers to their fullest, worked tirelessly to cleanse the ley lines, to break the network of dark energies. The battle was invisible to the naked eye, but its effects were profound.

As dawn broke, Maaya, standing at the heart of the city, felt a sense of peace and balance return to Lucknow. The natural disturbances ceased, and the city breathed a sigh of relief, unaware of the guardian who had protected them through the night.

The protector's resolve had been tested, and Maaya had emerged triumphant. She had faced one of her greatest challenges yet and had succeeded in preserving the harmony of the city she had sworn to protect.

As Maaya walked through the streets of Lucknow, she reflected on her journey. She had grown in strength and wisdom, her resolve as a guardian fortified by the challenges she had overcome. The path ahead would surely hold more trials, but Maaya was ready. She was the protector of Lucknow, a guardian of balance, and her resolve was unshakable.

Chapter 35: Legacy of the Ancients

In the calm that followed the restoration of Lucknow's ley lines, Maaya found herself delving deeper into the legacy of her guardianship. The recent challenges had not only tested her resolve but had also awakened a desire to understand the origins and history of the guardians. This quest for knowledge led her on a journey that intertwined her destiny with the ancient legacy she was a part of.

Guided by Anaya, Maaya began to explore the ancient texts and lore of the guardians. These texts, some written in forgotten languages, others in cryptic symbols, held the wisdom of generations of guardians who had walked the path before her. The knowledge contained within these pages was vast and profound, covering the mysteries of the natural world, the intricacies of energy manipulation, and the guardians' role in maintaining the balance between the seen and unseen.

As Maaya delved into these ancient teachings, she discovered that the guardians had been integral to many pivotal moments in history. They had silently influenced the course of events, working in the shadows to maintain harmony and prevent catastrophes. This revelation brought a new dimension to Maaya's understanding of her role, connecting her to a legacy that spanned millennia.

One of the most significant discoveries was the existence of a network of guardians across the world, each responsible for protecting a specific geographical area. This network, though loosely connected, shared a common purpose and occasionally came together to address global threats to the balance. Maaya realized that her actions in Lucknow were part of a larger tapestry of guardianship that encompassed the entire planet.

Emboldened by this knowledge, Maaya reached out to other guardians. Through a series of subtle communications, she made contact with guardians in different parts of the world. These interactions were enlightening, providing her with different perspectives on the challenges they faced and the strategies they employed.

One such interaction led to a crucial revelation about the dark energies she had been combating. These energies were not isolated incidents, but part of a larger scheme orchestrated by a shadowy figure known only as "The Adversary." This figure, shrouded in mystery, had been manipulating events to create imbalances in various parts of the world.

Armed with this knowledge, Maaya's mission became clearer. She needed to not only protect Lucknow but also to be part of the global effort to counteract The Adversary's plans. Her role as a guardian had expanded beyond the boundaries of her city, placing her at the forefront of a cosmic battle for balance.

As the academic year resumed, Maaya returned to the University of Lucknow with a renewed sense of purpose. Her studies, her role as a basketball player, and her environmental initiatives took on new meaning, each a facet of her guardianship. She approached her responsibilities with a wisdom and maturity that was a direct result of her deep dive into the legacy of the ancients.

The legacy of the ancients was not just a history; it was a living, breathing guide that shaped Maaya's path as a guardian. It connected her to a lineage of protectors, each contributing to the preservation of harmony in the world. As Maaya walked the campus, her connection to this legacy was a source of strength and inspiration, guiding her actions and reinforcing her resolve to uphold her duty as a guardian.

Chapter 36: Alliance Against Adversity

With the revelation of The Adversary's influence on a global scale, Maaya understood that the battles she faced in Lucknow were part of a much larger conflict. This understanding led her to strengthen her alliances with other guardians across the world. Recognizing the power of unity in the face of adversity, Maaya began to forge a network of allies, each committed to protecting the balance of the natural world.

This period of alliance-building was a time of learning and growth for Maaya. Through her interactions with other guardians, she gained insights into different cultures and traditions, each with its own approach to guardianship. These exchanges broadened her perspective and equipped her with new strategies and techniques to combat the disturbances caused by The Adversary.

One of the key allies Maaya connected with was Kaito, a guardian from Japan, whose expertise lay in harmonizing energy flows. Kaito's methods, rooted in ancient Shinto practices, provided Maaya with a different viewpoint on energy manipulation, one that emphasized harmony and flow over direct confrontation.

Another significant alliance was formed with Nia, a guardian from Kenya, who specialized in environmental preservation. Nia's deep connection to the natural world and her approach to ecological balance were invaluable to Maaya's efforts to restore and maintain the natural order in and around Lucknow.

As Maaya's network of allies grew, so did her influence and capability to address the challenges posed by The Adversary. The guardians began coordinating their efforts, sharing information and resources to counteract the disturbances and imbalances that were cropping up in different parts of the world.

Back in Lucknow, Maaya utilized the knowledge and techniques she gained from her alliances to strengthen the city's defences against supernatural disturbances. Alongside Aarav, she implemented measures to protect the ley lines and energy vortexes, ensuring that the city remained a bastion of balance and harmony.

The alliance against adversity also brought a new dynamic to Maaya's life at the university. She began to integrate the wisdom and practices she learned from her fellow guardians into her environmental initiatives, garnering appreciation and support from students and faculty alike.

However, the growing threat of The Adversary loomed large. Reports from other guardians indicated that The Adversary was orchestrating a series of events that could lead to a significant imbalance in the global energy grid. The implications of such an imbalance were dire, and the need for a coordinated response was urgent.

Maaya, now a key figure in the global network of guardians, found herself at the forefront of planning a strategy to counter The Adversary's schemes. Her journey from a solitary guardian in Lucknow to a leader in a global alliance was a testament to her growth and the respect she had earned from her peers.

As Maaya prepared to join forces with her fellow guardians in a concerted effort against The Adversary, she felt a mix of determination and apprehension. The challenges ahead were daunting, but she was not alone. She had the support and strength of her allies, each a guardian in their own right, united in their purpose to maintain the balance of the world.

The alliance against adversity was more than a coalition of

protectors; it was a symbol of hope and resilience, a unified front against the forces that sought to disrupt the harmony of the natural world. Maaya, at the heart of this alliance, stood ready to lead the charge, her resolve unwavering, her spirit indomitable.

Chapter 37: The Final Stand

As the threat posed by The Adversary grew more imminent, Maaya and her global network of guardians prepared for what they anticipated would be a decisive confrontation. The Final Stand, as it came to be known among the guardians, was not just a battle against a singular enemy, but a defence of the delicate balance that sustained life across the world.

The guardians converged from various parts of the globe, each bringing unique skills and perspectives to the alliance. Maaya, as a central figure in this coalition, worked tirelessly to coordinate their efforts, drawing on the strength and wisdom she had gained from her journey.

The Adversary's plan became clear through intelligence gathered by the guardians. A series of ancient artifacts, imbued with immense power, were to be used to create a global network of dark energy. This network, if activated, would disrupt the natural order, causing widespread chaos and imbalance. The guardians' mission was to prevent the activation of these artifacts and to neutralize The Adversary's influence.

The guardians split into teams, each tasked with locating and securing one of the artifacts. Maaya led one of the teams, her determination and resolve a beacon of inspiration for her allies. The mission took them to remote and dangerous locations, each artifact guarded by forces loyal to The Adversary.

In Lucknow, the final artifact lay hidden within the ancient catacombs beneath the city. Maaya, accompanied by Aarav and a group of guardians, ventured into the depths, aware that this would be the epicentre of The Adversary's scheme.

As they navigated the labyrinthine catacombs, they encountered fierce resistance. Shadowy entities and traps set by The Adversary hindered their progress. Maaya, drawing upon her full array of powers, led her team through each challenge, her focus unwavering.

Finally, they reached the chamber where the artifact was held. The energy in the chamber was oppressive, the artifact's dark power palpable. It was here that The Adversary revealed himself, a figure of menacing power, his presence a distortion in the fabric of reality.

The confrontation was intense, a culmination of the guardians' efforts to thwart The Adversary's plans. Maaya and her allies battled with all their might, their powers harmonized in a symphony of light against the darkness.

In the midst of the battle, Maaya realized that defeating The Adversary required more than just physical strength; it required a unity of spirit and purpose. Drawing on the collective energy of her allies, Maaya channelled a powerful surge of harmonious energy towards The Adversary.

The final moments of the battle were a clash of epic proportions. The chamber was filled with a blinding light as the harmonious energy collided with the dark power of The Adversary. In a moment that seemed to suspend time, the forces of balance and chaos met in a decisive explosion of energy.

When the light subsided, the guardians found themselves victorious. The Adversary had been vanquished; his plans thwarted. The artifact, now cleansed of its dark influence, was secured.

The Final Stand was not just a victory for the guardians; it was a reaffirmation of the strength that comes from unity and shared purpose. The alliance had triumphed against seemingly insurmountable odds, a testament to the power of collaboration in the face of adversity.

As the guardians emerged from the catacombs, the city of Lucknow, and indeed the world, breathed a sigh of relief. The balance had been restored; the natural order preserved.

Maaya, standing among her fellow guardians, felt a deep sense of accomplishment and pride. She had led the Final Stand, her journey as a guardian reaching a moment of triumph. The path ahead would undoubtedly hold more challenges, but Maaya was ready, her resolve strengthened, her purpose clearer than ever.

Chapter 38: Triumph of Light

In the wake of The Final Stand, the guardians' victory was felt not just in the physical realm, but in the very fabric of the natural order. The triumph over The Adversary marked a significant turning point in the battle to maintain the world's balance. For Maaya, this victory was a profound affirmation of her journey and the choices she had made along the way.

The aftermath of the battle saw the guardians disbanding, each returning to their respective parts of the world. However, the bonds formed during their struggle remained strong. They had become more than allies; they were a unified force, a global network of protectors ready to come together in times of need.

Maaya returned to Lucknow, where the impact of their victory was immediately apparent. The city felt rejuvenated, its energies harmonized. The disturbances that had plagued it were gone, replaced by a sense of peace and vitality. The people of Lucknow, unaware of the role Maaya had played, enjoyed the renewed spirit of their city.

At the University of Lucknow, Maaya resumed her studies and her environmental initiatives with a new vigor. The triumph over The Adversary had given her a deeper understanding of her powers and her role as a guardian. She approached her duties with a renewed sense of purpose, integrating the knowledge and experience she had gained from her allies into her efforts.

The university community noticed the change in Maaya. She was more confident, more driven, and her initiatives more impactful. Her work in environmental preservation and sustainability took on new dimensions, drawing inspiration from the global perspectives she had encountered.

Maaya's personal life also flourished in the aftermath of the victory. Her relationship with Aarav deepened, their bond strengthened by the trials they had faced together. Aarav's support and understanding had been invaluable, and Maaya knew that he would be a lifelong partner in her endeavors.

Her friendship with Priya, too, was rekindled. Maaya, now more open about her experiences, shared the lessons she had learned, albeit without revealing her secret identity. Priya, for her part, was just happy to have her friend back, her spirit unburdened.

The guardians' triumph over The Adversary was a victory for the light. It was a demonstration of the power of unity and the resilience of the natural order. For Maaya, it was a validation of her role as a guardian, a role that she now embraced with a full heart.

The triumph of light was not just the end of a battle; it was the beginning of a new era of guardianship. Maaya, with her enhanced abilities and deepened understanding, was at the forefront of this new era. She had emerged from the trials of her journey as a beacon of hope and a defender of the delicate balance that sustained life.

As Maaya looked towards the future, she did so with a sense of optimism and responsibility. She knew that there would be more challenges, more battles to fight. But she also knew that she was not alone. She had a network of guardians, a community of allies, and the strength of her convictions.

The Triumph of Light was a testament to Maaya's journey, a journey that had transformed her from a hesitant protector into a confident guardian of the world's balance. It was a journey that would continue, with Maaya leading the way, her light shining brightly in the darkness.

Chapter 39: Aftermath of War

The battle against The Adversary had ended, but its echoes resonated in the hearts and minds of those who had been a part of it. For Maaya, the aftermath of this war was a time of reflection and rebuilding, both personally and for the wider world she had fought to protect.

In the days following the victory, Maaya worked alongside her fellow guardians to repair the damages caused by the conflict. They focused on restoring the disrupted energy lines and healing the scars left in the natural world. This task, though less dramatic than the battle itself, was crucial in ensuring the long-term stability of the balance they had fought to maintain.

Back at the University of Lucknow, Maaya resumed her academic life, but the experience had changed her. She carried with her a deeper understanding of her role as a guardian and a heightened awareness of the interconnectedness of all things. Her studies, once a part of her everyday routine, now took on a new dimension, informed by her experiences and the knowledge she had gained from her fellow guardians.

Her environmental initiatives at the university became more influential. Drawing on the global network of guardians, Maaya introduced innovative practices and ideas that put the university at the forefront of sustainable living and environmental consciousness. These initiatives not only made a tangible impact on the campus but also served as a model for other institutions.

The aftermath of the war also brought a period of introspection for Maaya. She pondered the sacrifices made and the losses endured. The battle had been won, but it had come at a cost. Some guardians had fallen, their sacrifices a stark reminder of the stakes involved in their duty. Maaya honored their memory, vowing to continue their legacy of protection and balance.

Her relationships with Aarav and Priya also evolved. With Aarav, the bond had deepened, forged in the fires of conflict and strengthened by shared ideals and goals. With Priya, Maaya found a renewed connection, their friendship blossoming anew as Maaya shared more of her experiences and insights, though still guarding her secret identity as a guardian.

As the world slowly recovered from the effects of the battle, Maaya realized that the victory over The Adversary was not an end, but a milestone. The world was ever-changing, and the balance would always need guardians to protect it. Maaya embraced this reality, understanding that her journey would be a continuous one, filled with challenges and responsibilities.

The aftermath of war was a time of healing and growth. It was a period when the guardians strengthened their bonds and reaffirmed their commitment to their duty. For Maaya, it was a chapter that closed one phase of her journey and opened another, her resolve and dedication to her role as a guardian stronger than ever.

Chapter 40: Rebuilding and Reflection

In the tranquility that followed the tumultuous events of the war, Maaya engaged in a period of rebuilding and reflection. This phase was crucial for her, as it allowed her to consolidate her experiences and prepare for the continuous journey ahead as a guardian.

The University of Lucknow, having become a focal point of Maaya's efforts, underwent a transformation. The environmental initiatives that Maaya spearheaded, influenced by her experiences and the global network of guardians, began to bear fruit. The campus blossomed into a model of sustainability, its practices and ethos inspiring other institutions and communities.

For Maaya, the process of rebuilding was not just physical but also emotional. The battles she had fought had left their mark. She took time to process her experiences, understanding that the path of a guardian was fraught with emotional as well as physical challenges. This introspection helped her come to terms with the sacrifices made and the lessons learned.

Her mentor, Anaya, played a crucial role during this period. Anaya's wisdom and guidance helped Maaya navigate the complexities of her role, providing a sounding board for her thoughts and emotions. These discussions deepened Maaya's understanding of her responsibilities and the impact of her actions on the world.

The rebuilding phase also saw Maaya strengthening her bonds with her allies. Aarav, who had been a constant support, became an integral part of Maaya's efforts at the university and in the broader environmental initiatives. Their partnership was a blend of professional collaboration and personal support, grounded in shared values and goals.

Priya, too, remained an important part of Maaya's life. Their friendship, resilient and enduring, provided Maaya with a sense of normalcy and connection. While Priya was unaware of Maaya's secret identity, the trust and understanding between them were unwavering, a reminder of the importance of human connections in Maaya's life.

The reflection phase allowed Maaya to look back on her journey and appreciate the growth she had undergone. From a hesitant newcomer to the guardians' world to a confident and capable protector, Maaya had transformed. She recognized that her journey was a continuous learning process, one where each experience, each challenge, brought new insights and strengthened her resolve.

As the academic year progressed, Maaya's initiatives and leadership at the university garnered recognition. She became a symbol of change and progress, her efforts a testament to the power of dedication and vision.

However, Maaya knew that the role of a guardian was never static. The world was an ever-changing tapestry of energies, and the balance she strove to protect would always be subject to shifts and disturbances. Ready to face future challenges, Maaya looked forward with a sense of purpose and optimism, her experiences during the war shaping her approach to guardianship.

The period of rebuilding and reflection was a necessary respite, a time to gather strength and wisdom for the path ahead. Maaya emerged from it more grounded and focused, her commitment to her role as a guardian reaffirmed and her spirit renewed.

Chapter 41: New Horizons

As the academic year drew to a close at the University of Lucknow, Maaya found herself at a crossroads. The time of rebuilding and reflection had been fruitful, allowing her to integrate the lessons learned from her recent battles into her life as a student, environmentalist, and guardian. Now, she stood ready to embrace new horizons, both in her personal journey and her continuing role as a protector of balance.

Maaya's experiences had attracted the attention of environmental organizations beyond the university. Recognizing her leadership and innovative approaches, they invited her to contribute to larger-scale sustainability projects. This opportunity to expand her impact was both exciting and daunting, but Maaya saw it as a natural progression of her journey.

Simultaneously, Maaya's role as a guardian took on a new dimension. The network of guardians she had helped forge was now a robust global entity, capable of responding to threats to the natural balance more effectively. As part of this network, Maaya's responsibilities expanded beyond the confines of Lucknow, positioning her as a key figure in the guardians' collective efforts.

This expansion of her role required Maaya to travel, to meet with other guardians, and to engage in collaborative efforts to address environmental and supernatural disturbances. Each journey brought new challenges and learnings, further enhancing her skills and understanding of her role as a guardian.

Despite the broadening scope of her responsibilities, Maaya remained grounded in her roots. Lucknow, with its rich heritage and the University, continued to be her home base, a place where she could recharge and reflect. Her relationships with Aarav and Priya remained central to her life, providing stability and emotional support.

Aarav, in particular, became a partner not just in her environmental endeavors but also in her broader mission as a guardian. His knowledge and perspective were invaluable, and their partnership evolved into a powerful force for positive change.

The new horizons also brought personal growth for Maaya. She matured into a confident leader, her experiences shaping her approach to challenges and decision-making. Her journey as a guardian had taught her the importance of balance, not just in the natural world but in her personal life as well.

As she embarked on these new endeavors, Maaya's sense of purpose was stronger than ever. She understood that her journey was not just about protecting the present but also about shaping a sustainable future. Her role as a guardian had become an integral part of her identity, a guiding force in her efforts to make a positive impact on the world.

The horizon ahead was vast and filled with possibilities. Maaya approached it with a sense of optimism and determination, ready to face the challenges and seize the opportunities that lay ahead. Her journey had taken her from a hesitant newcomer to a confident guardian, and now to a leader and innovator in the quest for balance and harmony.

Chapter 42: The Protector's Network

Embracing the new horizons that lay before her, Maaya's journey as a guardian evolved into a role that transcended geographical boundaries. The Protector's Network, a global alliance of guardians that she had helped forge, became a pivotal part of her life, facilitating collaboration and action on a scale she had never before imagined.

The network was a testament to the unity and strength of guardians worldwide. It served as a platform for sharing knowledge, coordinating responses to global threats, and supporting each other in their individual struggles to maintain balance. For Maaya, the network was not just a resource; it was a family of like-minded individuals who shared her commitment and her challenges.

As part of the Protector's Network, Maaya embarked on missions that took her to different parts of the world. Each mission was a learning experience, exposing her to diverse cultures, environments, and challenges. She worked alongside other guardians, each bringing their unique abilities and perspectives to the table, creating a formidable force against disturbances to the natural order.

One such mission took Maaya to the Amazon rainforest, where she and a team of guardians worked to counteract a severe disruption in the ecological balance. The experience was eye-opening, highlighting the interconnectedness of all life and the far-reaching impact of human actions on the environment.

Back in Lucknow, Maaya leveraged her experiences and the connections within the Protector's Network to enhance her local initiatives. Her work at the University of Lucknow and in the city gained new depth, influenced by the global perspectives and strategies she had encountered.

The network also provided Maaya with emotional support. Being a guardian was a demanding role, often fraught with danger and moral dilemmas. The camaraderie and understanding within the network were invaluable, giving Maaya a sense of belonging and a forum to share her experiences and challenges.

Aarav, who had become an integral part of Maaya's journey, played a key role in integrating the global insights into their local projects. His analytical mind and deep understanding of environmental science were assets that greatly enhanced their efforts.

Priya, Maaya's steadfast friend, although not privy to the full extent of Maaya's role, sensed the positive changes in her. Their friendship continued to be a source of joy and grounding for Maaya, a reminder of the importance of human connections amidst her responsibilities as a guardian.

The Protector's Network was more than a coalition of guardians; it was a symbol of hope and a force for good. It represented the collective strength of individuals united by a common purpose, transcending borders and cultures.

For Maaya, being part of this network was a reaffirmation of her path as a guardian. It bolstered her resolve to face the challenges ahead and strengthened her belief in the power of unity and collaboration. The network was a beacon, guiding her as she navigated the complexities of her role, and supporting her in her continued efforts to protect the balance of the world.

Chapter 43: A Beacon of Hope

Maaya's involvement in the Protector's Network had elevated her role as a guardian to a global stage. Her efforts, both locally in Lucknow and as part of the network, began to resonate far beyond her immediate surroundings. Maaya had become a beacon of hope, an emblem of the guardians' fight for balance and harmony in a world increasingly fraught with challenges.

In this new role, Maaya found herself at the forefront of significant initiatives. One such initiative was a global campaign to raise awareness about environmental degradation and the importance of preserving natural balance. Maaya's voice, along with those of her fellow guardians, reached a wide audience, spreading a message of responsibility and action.

Her work took her to international conferences and forums, where she spoke not just as a guardian, but as a young leader passionate about creating a sustainable future. Her insights, drawn from her experiences as a guardian and her academic background, were influential in shaping discussions and policies.

Back at the University of Lucknow, Maaya's achievements were a source of pride and inspiration. She had become a role model for students and faculty alike, embodying the ideals of dedication, courage, and commitment to a greater cause. Her environmental initiatives on campus continued to thrive, now bolstered by her global experiences and connections.

Despite her growing prominence, Maaya remained grounded. She continued to value the personal connections that had supported her throughout her journey. Her relationship with Aarav was a partnership of equals, each supporting and enhancing the other's efforts. Aarav's unwavering support and shared commitment to environmental causes made him not just a partner in her initiatives but also in her life.

Maaya's friendship with Priya remained a constant in her ever-evolving world. Priya's presence provided a sense of normalcy and comfort, a reminder of the life Maaya had outside her responsibilities as a guardian. Their bond, strengthened by years of shared experiences, was a testament to the enduring power of friendship.

As a beacon of hope, Maaya's influence extended beyond environmental activism and guardianship. She became a symbol of what could be achieved when passion, dedication, and a sense of responsibility converged. Young people, in particular, were drawn to her story, seeing in her a reflection of their own potential to make a difference in the world.

The role of a guardian, as Maaya had learned, was multifaceted. It was not just about combating threats to the natural balance but also about inspiring and leading others towards a path of sustainability and harmony. Maaya embraced this role wholeheartedly, using her position to advocate for change and to inspire action.

As she looked towards the future, Maaya saw a world brimming with possibilities. The challenges were many, but so were the opportunities to make a meaningful impact. Her journey as a guardian had taught her that every action, no matter how small, contributed to the greater good.

Maaya's story, from a hesitant newcomer to a beacon of hope, was a journey of transformation. It was a journey that spoke of the power of individual commitment and the collective strength of those united for a common cause. Maaya stood as a guardian, a leader, and a symbol of hope, her light shining brightly in a world that needed it more than ever.

Chapter 44: Legacy of Maaya Lakshmi

As years passed, Maaya Lakshmi's legacy continued to grow, both as a guardian of the natural world and as an inspiring figure in the realm of environmental activism. Her journey, marked by challenges, triumphs, and continuous growth, had become a story that resonated with people far and wide, transcending cultural and geographical boundaries.

Maaya's impact on the University of Lucknow remained indelible. The environmental initiatives she had spearheaded transformed the campus into a model of sustainability, inspiring other educational institutions to follow suit. Students who had worked with her carried the lessons learned into their own careers and lives, spreading Maaya's vision and ethos.

Nationally and internationally, Maaya's contributions to environmental awareness and guardianship had made her a respected figure in the global community. Her involvement in high-level discussions on sustainability and her role in the Protector's Network positioned her as a key influencer in shaping policies and practices related to environmental balance and conservation.

Throughout her journey, Maaya had maintained her connections with those who had been instrumental in her growth. Aarav, now her partner in both life and work, continued to support and complement her efforts. Their partnership was a fusion of love, respect, and shared commitment to making a positive impact on the world.

Priya, ever the steadfast friend, remained a grounding influence in Maaya's life. Their friendship, enduring through the years, was a testament to the power of human connection and loyalty.

Priya's unwavering support had been a source of strength for Maaya, reminding her of the importance of maintaining personal relationships amid her larger responsibilities.

As Maaya reflected on her journey, she realized that her legacy was not just in the battles fought or the initiatives led; it was in the inspiration she had provided to others. She had shown that one individual's commitment and courage could effect meaningful change. Her story was a catalyst for others to take up the mantle of guardianship and activism in their own ways.

Maaya's legacy also lay in the continuation of the Protector's Network, which had grown into a formidable force for the protection of the natural world. The network, guided by the principles Maaya had helped establish, continued to work tirelessly to maintain the balance between the natural and supernatural realms.

In her quieter moments, Maaya often pondered the path she had taken. From a young student uncertain of her place in the world to a guardian and leader, her journey had been extraordinary. She had faced adversities, embraced her destiny, and emerged as a symbol of hope and resilience.

Maaya Lakshmi's legacy was multifaceted – it was a legacy of environmental stewardship, of guardianship over the natural balance, and of inspiring others to be agents of change. As she looked towards the future, Maaya knew that her journey was far from over. There would always be challenges to face and new horizons to explore.

Her story, a blend of mythology and reality, of battles fought and wisdom gained, would continue to inspire future generations. Maaya Lakshmi, the guardian of balance, the environmentalist, the beacon of hope, had left an indelible mark on the world, a legacy that would endure long after her time.

EPILOGUE: THE GUARDIAN'S LEGACY

Years had passed since Maaya Lakshmi first embraced her destiny as a guardian of balance. The city of Lucknow, once a stage for her early battles, had flourished under her watch, its harmony a testament to her enduring vigil.

Now, in the twilight of her journey, Maaya stood on the banks of the Gomti River, her gaze reflecting the wisdom and experiences of a lifetime. The river flowed ceaselessly, a symbol of the eternal dance between order and chaos, a dance she had been a part of.

Beside her stood a young girl, her eyes wide with the boundless curiosity of youth. She was Maaya's protégé, chosen to continue the legacy that Maaya had upheld for so many years. In her, Maaya saw the same spark that had ignited her own path so many years ago.

"Will I be able to do it, to be a guardian like you?" the young girl asked, her voice tinged with awe and uncertainty.

Maaya turned to her, a gentle smile playing on her lips. "You will," she said, her voice soft yet firm. "The path of a guardian is challenging and filled with trials. But it is also a path of growth, of discovering your strength and the power of unity."

The sun dipped below the horizon, casting a golden glow over the river. Maaya's eyes turned towards the horizon, her thoughts reaching back to the journey she had traversed.
"There will be times of doubt and fear," Maaya continued, her gaze returning to the young girl. "But remember, the power of a guardian lies not in battling darkness alone, but in nurturing the light within and around you."

The young girl listened, absorbing every word, her resolve

strengthening.

Maaya reached out, placing a gentle hand on the girl's shoulder. "My journey began with a vision, a calling to a destiny larger than I had ever imagined. Now, as my path converges with the twilight, I pass the torch to you. You are the new guardian, the new beacon of hope."

As the night embraced the world, the torch of guardianship passed to a new bearer. Maaya Lakshmi's legacy would live on, not just in the stories and the change she had brought to the world, but in the heart of a new guardian, ready to embark on her own journey. Maaya's tale had been one of courage, wisdom, and unwavering commitment. A tale that would inspire generations, reminding them of the delicate balance that sustains life, and of the guardians who stand watch, ever vigilant, ever protective.

In the whispers of the wind, in the rustling of the leaves, and in the flow of the river, her legacy would endure, a guardian not just of nature, but of the hope and strength that dwells within us all.

"Maaya Lakshmi will return in
The Guardian's Odyssey"

The Divine Awakening